"Why don't you lie down?" Mark said. "I'll be right back."

As he turned to go, Juliet grabbed the sleeve of his shirt, her rich mahogany eyes snaring his, setting his nerves on edge, making his heart rumble in his chest.

"Thanks...for...you know." She gave a little shrug. "For everything."

"No problem." But as he stepped into the crisp, cool morning air, he wasn't so sure he'd done anything commendable. After all, Juliet wasn't in the hospital—where she belonged.

And Mark, who had volunteered to be her private-duty nurse, didn't know anything about pregnant women, childbirth or babies.

What in the hell had he set himself up for?

Dear Reader,

Celebrate those April showers this month by curling up inside with a good book—and we at Silhouette Special Edition are happy to start you off with *What's Cooking?* by Sherryl Woods, the next in her series THE ROSE COTTAGE SISTERS. When a playboy photographer is determined to seduce a beautiful food critic fed up with men who won't commit…things *really* start to heat up! In Judy Duarte's *Their Unexpected Family,* next in our MONTANA MAVERICKS: GOLD RUSH GROOMS continuity, a very pregnant—not to mention, single—small-town waitress and a globe-trotting reporter find themselves drawn to each other despite their obvious differences. Stella Bagwell concludes THE FORTUNES OF TEXAS: REUNION with *In a Texas Minute.* A woman who has finally found the baby of her dreams to adopt lacks the one element that can make it happen—a husband—or *does* she? She's suddenly looking at her handsome "best friend" in a new light. Christine Flynn begins her new GOING HOME miniseries—which centers around a small Vermont town—with *Trading Secrets,* in which a down-but-not-out native repairs to her hometown to get over her heartbreak…and falls smack into the arms of the town's handsome new doctor. *Least Likely Wedding?* by Patricia McLinn, the first in her SOMETHING OLD, SOMETHING NEW… series, features a lovely filmmaker whose "groom" on celluloid is all too eager to assume the role in real life. And in *The Million Dollar Cowboy* by Judith Lyons, a woman who's fallen hard for a cowboy has to convince him to take a chance on love.

So don't let those April showers get you down! May is just around the corner—and with it, six fabulous new reads, all from Silhouette Special Edition.

Happy reading!

Gail Chasan
Senior Editor

Please address questions and book requests to:
Silhouette Reader Service
U.S.: 3010 Walden Ave., P.O. Box 1325, Buffalo, NY 14269
Canadian: P.O. Box 609, Fort Erie, Ont. L2A 5X3

THEIR
UNEXPECTED FAMILY

JUDY DUARTE

Silhouette

SPECIAL EDITION

Published by Silhouette Books

America's Publisher of Contemporary Romance

Special thanks and acknowledgment are given to Judy Duarte for her contribution
to the MONTANA MAVERICKS: GOLD RUSH GROOMS series.

To Emalee Rae Colwell, who made her appearance in time to give Grandma
a refresher course on birthing rooms and the miracle of childbirth.
Welcome to the world, baby girl!

In addition, I'd like to thank Christine Rimmer, Allison Leigh, Pamela Toth,
Karen Rose Smith and Cheryl St.John, the other authors of this
Montana Mavericks series, for making this book a pleasure to write.

 SILHOUETTE BOOKS

ISBN 0-373-24676-5

THEIR UNEXPECTED FAMILY

Visit Silhouette Books at www.eHarlequin.com

Printed in U.S.A.

Books by Judy Duarte

Silhouette Special Edition

Cowboy Courage #1458
Family Practice #1511
Almost Perfect #1540
Big Sky Baby #1563
The Virgin's Makeover #1593
Bluegrass Baby #1598
The Rich Man's Son #1634
Hailey's Hero #1659
Their Secret Son #1667
Their Unexpected Family #1676

Silhouette Books

Double Destiny
"Second Chance"

JUDY DUARTE

An avid reader who enjoys a happy ending, Judy Duarte always wanted to write books of her own. One day she decided to make that dream come true. Five years and six manuscripts later, she sold her first book to Silhouette Special Edition.

Her unpublished stories have won the Emily and the Orange Rose, and in 2001, she became a double Golden Heart finalist. Judy credits her success to Romance Writers of America and two wonderful critique partners, Sheri WhiteFeather and Crystal Green, both of whom write for Silhouette.

At times, when a stubborn hero and a headstrong heroine claim her undivided attention, she and her family are thankful for fast food, pizza delivery and video games. When she's not at the keyboard or in a Walter Mitty–type world, she enjoys traveling, spending romantic evenings with her personal hero and playing board games with her kids.

Judy lives in Southern California and loves to hear from her readers. You may write to her at: P.O. Box 498, San Luis Rey, CA 92068-0498. You can also visit her Web site at www.judyduarte.com.

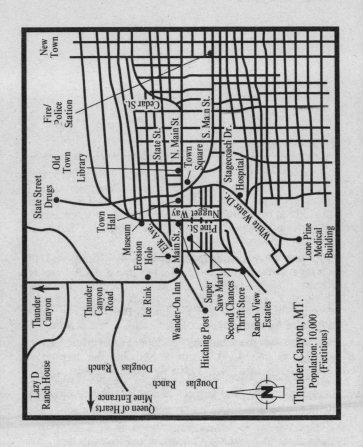

New Town

Fire/Police Station

Cedar St.

State St.

N. Main St

S. Main St.

Town Square

State Street Drugs

Old Town Library

Stagecoach Dr.

Hospital

White Water Dr.

Town Hall

Elk Ave.

Nugget Way

Lone Pine Medical Building

Museum

Erosion Hole

Pine St.

Main St.

Thunder Canyon

Thunder Canyon Road

Ice Rink

Wander-On Inn

Super Save Mart

Second Chances Thrift Store

Ranch View Estates

Lazy D Ranch House

Douglas Ranch

Hitching Post

Douglas Ranch

Queen of Hearts Mine Entrance

N

Thunder Canyon, MT.

Population: 10,000 (Fictitious)

Chapter One

Juliet Rivera had always favored the aroma of grilled onions and green peppers, but tonight, the kitchen smells of the busy bar and grill triggered a wave of nausea.

"Are those fries up yet?" she asked, arching her back and trailing her fingers along the contour of her distended womb.

God, she hoped everything was all right. The baby had been unusually quiet today, which increased her concern about working after Dr. Hart had recommended she take it easy. She didn't want to risk triggering premature labor, but she needed to support herself and the child she was going to bear.

Buck Crowley, the burly cook who'd once practiced his culinary skills on navy seamen, slid the plate toward her and grumbled. "You tell that fortune hunter that I'm not making them any crisper than this. French fries aren't supposed to be as hard as matchsticks."

"Thanks, Buck." Juliet made her way through the dining room of The Hitching Post and placed the well-done fries in front of the lanky customer who'd asked her to take them back to the kitchen.

She watched him poke a finger at the heaping platter of extra-crispy potato strips, apparently checking to see if they were made the way he'd requested.

He wasn't going to send them back again, was he?

If he did, she could imagine Buck storming out of the kitchen and into the dining room. The retired military man wasn't prone to confrontations with the customers, but he, along with some of the other Thunder Canyon locals, didn't appreciate all the strangers who'd flocked to the charming Montana town with hopes of striking it rich.

Years ago, several other gold rushes had lured their share of prospectors into Thunder Canyon. But the Queen of Hearts mine had played out, and Buck believed the contemporary gold-seekers would end up disappointed.

Juliet crossed her arms over the shelf her belly made and shifted her weight to one foot, waiting for the customer's approval.

Dios mio, señor. Cual es su problema? With just under six weeks to go until her due date, she'd probably give birth before he decided whether the fries were good enough.

Juliet was dead on her feet and ready to clock out,

especially after her visit to the emergency room two days ago. But she couldn't leave yet. The Hitching Post was hopping like a Saturday night, and it was only the middle of the week.

The persnickety customer finally shrugged his shoulders, then reached for a fry. When he popped a second one into his mouth, she turned to go, pausing as her boss approached.

Martha Tasker, a matronly woman who wore her silver-streaked hair pulled into a topknot, placed a hand on Juliet's shoulder. "I'm worried about you. How's it going?"

Other than sore feet and a twinge of nausea whenever she neared the kitchen? Juliet forced a smile. "I'm fine. Thanks."

"No more fainting spells?"

"Not since Sunday afternoon."

Mrs. Tasker studied her, as though trying to make her own assessment. "This is your just first night back on the job. We can try to handle the load without you. Why don't you call it quits until tomorrow?"

Because Juliet's small nest egg was only enough to see her through delivery and a few weeks after that. What would she do when it was gone? She'd been told there would be a workman's compensation settlement that would go to her brother's estate, but that could take years, and she wasn't counting on it.

She flashed her employer another smile, one she hoped boasted more confidence than she felt. "As soon as the dinner crowd thins out, I'll go home."

"Good," Mrs. Tasker said, as she began to wind her

way back to the cash register she manned. "We don't want that baby comin' into the world too early. That fainting spell nearly gave me a heart attack."

"*What* fainting spell?" a husky baritone voice asked.

Juliet glanced over her shoulder and spotted Mark Anderson, a reporter for a major news service who'd been sent to Thunder Canyon to cover the gold rush. Apparently, he'd just entered the dining room and had overheard her conversation with Mrs. Tasker.

She guessed him to be just shy of six feet, although he looked monstrously tall with his hands on his hips and glaring at her like a highway patrolman who'd just snagged a reckless driver. His dark hair, a bit long and unruly, bore a tinge of gray at the temples, so she judged him to be in his late thirties.

"It was nothing," she told him, although the fainting spell and ambulance ride to the hospital had been pretty scary.

The reporter eyed her carefully. "Have you seen a doctor?"

Juliet wasn't sure why he asked, why he cared. But she couldn't see any reason not to answer honestly. There were too many people in this world who didn't tell the truth, people who kept secrets. And she'd be darned if she'd be one of them. "I have a doctor. And I saw a resident obstetrician in the emergency room at Thunder Canyon General. Everything is fine, although I'm supposed to take it easy."

"Then what are you doing here?" His husky voice, with the hint of a soft southern drawl, settled over her like a drizzle of melted chocolate. But his probing eyes weren't nearly as sweet and comforting.

A strand of hair that had come loose from the gold clip she wore while at work tickled her cheek, and she swiped it away with the back of her hand. "What does it look like I'm doing?"

"You're certainly not taking it easy." His whiskey-brown eyes swept over her again, no doubt spotting the exhaustion in her expression that a dab of lipstick and mascara couldn't hide.

She wasn't sure whether she should be angry with him for butting in or pleased that he gave a darn about her health and the baby's welfare. But for a woman who'd grown up in a small, close-knit family, she'd been alone and on her own for too long to completely shrug off his concern.

He pulled out a chair and sat at the nearest table—on the dining room side, rather than closer to the bar where he usually parked himself for the evening. His gaze lingered on her, and he continued to study her with more interest than any of the other male customers.

At one time, she might have wondered if the reporter found her attractive. But how loco was that? With a belly that seemed to grow bigger every day, there wasn't much for a man to find appealing—not that she cared anyway. Her baby was the one and only priority in her life.

Wanting to break the intimacy of his gaze, to distance herself from his interest, she asked, "Can I get you something to eat?"

"Not yet. But I'll have a drink."

Since coming into town last week on assignment, he'd had several stiff shots of bourbon every night— at least, that's what he'd ordered when she'd been working. Then he ate dinner before heading across the street to the inn, where the news service had put him up.

She doubted he had a drinking problem, since his cynical yet flirtatious personality remained constant, and he appeared unaffected by his alcohol consumption.

"Bourbon and a splash of water?" she asked.

"Good memory."

"Predictable customer."

He grinned, and she headed for the bar, which sat on the far side of the room, near the dance floor that saw a lot of action on Friday and Saturday nights.

The Hitching Post had once been the town saloon, and although renovated many years ago into a respectable eatery, its history lingered in the old photographs that dotted the walls, the refurbished bar that still boasted scars and scratches from yesteryear and a painting of a nude woman, who was rumored to have been the original owner—the Shady Lady, as the locals called her.

Juliet always found it difficult not to stare at the image of the voluptuous blonde who sported a teasing grin. More straitlaced folks might disagree, but she thought the nineteenth-century piece of art added to the charm of The Hitching Post.

When the bartender handed her Mark's drink, she

returned to his table, placed a cocktail napkin in front of him, then served the glass of nearly straight bourbon.

He lifted his drink in a mock salute. "Thanks."

"You're welcome."

His eyes continued to study her, but she couldn't seem to make herself move, get back to work.

"Can you take a break?" he asked.

If she were inclined to think like a single woman on the prowl rather than an expectant mother wanting to nest, she'd consider it. "No, I'd better not. I'm still on the clock."

"There are laws about companies giving their employees a break during the workday." He glanced at her tummy, then caught her eyes in a mesmerizing gaze.

Juliet's grandmother, *Abuelita,* had taught her to search a person's expression —especially the eyes— to try and spot the secrets one kept. Of course, with Juliet's history, she wasn't very good at character assessment. And for some reason, she suspected she'd be just as lousy at guessing what drove Mark Anderson, what caused him to mellow out at night with alcohol instead of a cup of decaf and a slice of pie.

"Excuse me. I'd better get back to work." She turned to go, but he caught her by the hand.

Mark wasn't sure what had compelled him to touch the pretty Latina with sparkling caramel-colored eyes and long black hair she'd swept into a twist. It wasn't like him to be forward, but he'd been drawn to her since the first day he'd stepped into The Hitching Post hoping to while away the hours until his story developed.

Sure, there was a little attraction involved, he supposed. She was a beautiful woman, in spite of her condition. And her spunky personality made him sit up and take notice. But it was more than a case of Latin blood and genetics that caught his eye and held his interest.

He loosened his grip on her wrist, letting her go. "It wouldn't hurt for you to sit down for a while."

"I shouldn't," she said, but slowly took a seat anyway. "It's almost time for me to go home."

Mark couldn't remember any Hispanic families in the area when he'd lived in Thunder Canyon. But that had been twenty years ago.

"Where's home?" he asked.

She nodded at the ceiling. "I live here. In the apartment upstairs."

He hadn't expected her to reveal more than an "I live northeast of town," or "In that new housing development off White Water Drive." The women he knew liked to play cat-and-mouse games, never saying what was really on their minds, holding back and not revealing too much.

Was Juliet that young and inexperienced? Or were there a few women in this world who were still honest and open?

Either way, he found her innocence refreshing, to say the least.

He glanced at the ceiling, as she had done, and a grin tugged at his lips. "Did you know that the second floor of The Hitching Post used to be a whore-house?"

She smiled, a flush coloring her cheeks. "Mrs. Tasker, my boss and landlady, told me that, although she referred to it as a 'house of ill repute.' But you'd never know it now. One of the previous owners converted the upstairs into a living area for his family back in the 1950s."

Mark had heard the second floor was now an apartment. But when he'd lived in Thunder Canyon as a teenager, legends of the saloon and whorehouse held more interest for him and his friends than the renovations had.

"I lucked out," she told him. "I got a job and a place to live all in one day."

Lucky for her, maybe. Mark was glad he'd left Thunder Canyon. And just being within city limits made him uneasy and gave him reason to throw back a couple of bourbons before turning in, The booze helped pass the time and keep the memories at bay.

She shot him an unabashed grin. "I love it here."

"Here?" He scanned the dining room.

"Yes, working at The Hitching Post and living in Thunder Canyon, especially the old part of town. I love the Wild West charm."

Mark chuckled. "What are you, a history buff?"

"In a way." She fiddled with the unused napkin in front of her. "My dad and brother used to love those old shoot-'em-up westerns. You know, *Bonanza* reruns, *Gunsmoke*. John Wayne movies. And before long, I was hooked, too."

"Really?"

She leaned forward, her eyes flashing impishly, and grinned. "And when the TV is on the blink, I'm a big fan of Zane Grey and Louis L'Amour."

"No kidding?"

She lifted up her right hand in a Boy Scout fashion. "Honest. But don't tell." She smiled again, suggesting that she didn't really care what people thought of her choice of reading material. Caramel-colored flecks sparkled in her brown eyes. "On my days off, I walk along the wooden sidewalk here in Old Town and study the false-front buildings." She slid him an enchanting smile. "Sometimes, if I close my eyes, I can see a cowboy in a spun woolen shirt, leather vest and dungarees, walking along the dusty western streets."

"You don't say. That's a pretty vivid imagination you've got. Do you hear his spurs go jingle jangle jingle?"

"Of course." The mirth in her voice taunted his cynical nature. "You mean you haven't ever envisioned a prim lady dressed in calico and wearing a splash of lemon verbena?"

"No. Never." He leaned back in his chair, extending his legs, as his gaze swept her pretty face. "Not even a pretty *señorita* with flashing dark eyes."

Her lips, with only the hint of rose-colored lipstick, quirked as she made a tsk-tsk sound. "That's too bad. Life must be boring for a man mired in reality."

That was for sure. What little imagination Mark had was spent deciphering puzzles, weeding out lies and digging for the meat of a story. And although his life was normally far from dull, that wasn't the case on this assignment.

Covering the gold rush was a waste of his time, and it chapped his hide that his boss had sent him here because he'd once been a local boy. But Mark was a professional. He'd get the damn story written, make Thunder Canyon look remotely interesting, then get the hell out of town. As long as he could stay a step ahead of the memories he'd like to forget, he'd come out on top.

"My life isn't dull," he told her. "Not by a long shot. But I've got to admit I'm bored in Thunder Canyon."

She leaned back in her chair. "You're a stick in the mud."

"And you're a romantic."

Her smile drifted and the light in her eyes faded. "About some things, I suppose."

His gaze fell to her belly, to the swollen womb where her baby grew, and he realized the conversation had taken a personal turn for her. A heavy turn?

"What's your husband do?" he asked, curious about the guy and hoping he was supportive and making sure she didn't do too much in her condition.

"I'm not married. I'll be raising my child alone."

God knew he didn't want to go *there*. Mark would be in and out of town long before she had the baby. At least that was his game plan.

"Soooo," he said, trying to get them both back to an impersonal level, at least when it came to the lover in her past. "You fell in love with Thunder Canyon and settled here."

She nodded.

"Amazing. And I couldn't get out of town fast enough." The minute the words slipped out, he wanted to take them back.

There were some things Mark Anderson was hell-bent to forget, some memories he refused to discuss. Some guilt, that if left unchecked, would stealthily creep back in the dark of night, pointing a finger and reminding him how he'd failed his sister, his family.

But he'd be damned if he'd let the reminder haunt his dreams tonight. So he gamely changed the subject. *Again.* Back to *her* past. "Where are you from?"

"Originally? San Diego."

"That's a long way from Thunder Canyon."

"The distance was part of the appeal."

Mark nodded, as though he knew something he couldn't possibly understand. The reporter in him wanted to question her, to learn why she was running, but this wasn't another work-related interview. And he didn't want to encourage self-disclosure when turnabout *wasn't* fair play.

"My baby's father didn't want our child," she offered without being asked, then shrugged and cast a smile that didn't convince Mark that the guy's rejection hadn't done a number on her. "So I left town with the intent of settling down in the first place that felt like home to me."

The lover who'd fathered her baby was a fool. But Mark kept the thought to himself. "And you just ended up here?"

"I stopped at a restaurant near Sacramento and

chatted with a couple of tourists who'd come from Montana. They told me how quaint and charming Thunder Canyon was, and I decided to visit."

"And then you decided to stay." An easy assumption.

"That's about the size of it." She scooted her chair back and stood, her belly and the baby stretching between them.

"Where are you going?" he asked.

"Back to work."

"Shouldn't you go upstairs and put your feet up or something?" He didn't know why he was feeling so protective of her.

God knew he didn't have any intention of getting involved with any local women, not to mention a pregnant one who was a good ten to fifteen years younger than he was. But that didn't keep him from feeling sorry for her. After all, the father of her child wasn't in the picture, and considering her job, money was obviously an issue.

She shouldn't be working so hard this late in her pregnancy. Something could go wrong.

A momentary flash—lightning quick—thundered in his chest, reverberating in his mind and threatening to shake the memories free from their dark hiding place.

Kelly lying on the floor. The gray pallor of her death mask. The distended belly. The pool of blood.

Mark could tap dance around the truth all night. But he knew where the urge to protect the pretty waitress had come from.

His sister had been about Juliet's age when she and her unborn son had died.

As Juliet slid the chair she'd been sitting in back to the table, obviously ending their chat and the short break she'd taken, he couldn't keep quiet. "I hope you're turning in your apron for the evening."

"Dr. Hart told me to take it easy. And she suggested I stop work. But that's not an option right now."

"You need to take the doctor's orders more seriously." No one understood how something could go wrong better than Mark.

"I did take the doctor seriously. I took off two days from work, I've cut back my hours a bit and the other waitresses have tried to make my job easier."

Before Mark could stop her, she made her way to another table, leaving him to ponder the easy banter, the subtle flirtation that went on despite her circumstances.

And the overwhelming urge to take care of a woman he hardly knew.

He took a drink of the bourbon. And then another. He hoped the alcohol would drown the memories Juliet's pregnancy had invoked. But it didn't seem likely.

The godawful guilt had reared its head, and it was too late to turn back the clock, to right a wrong he'd never forget.

Chapter Two

As was his custom, at least while in Thunder Canyon, Mark ended each day of interviews by downing a couple of drinks and having dinner at The Hitching Post.

He didn't feel any better about the value of his work on this story or feel any closer to wrapping it up than he had on his first day back in town. For the most part, all he could come up with was human-interest type stuff.

Public opinion, it seemed, was split when it came to the gold rush and the influx of fortune hunters.

Some townspeople had gotten so excited by the fervor, they'd locked up their homes and drained their bank accounts in order to buy prospecting gear. Others—mostly business owners—were pleased by the increase in revenue the newcomers brought to town.

But then there were the vocal locals, those who hated the publicity and the swarm of strangers who'd turned the quaint little town topsy-turvy. Juliet, with her love of history, probably fell into that group.

Mark scanned the room and found her near the cash register, talking to her boss. Why didn't Martha Tasker trade jobs and let the pregnant waitress sit on a stool while collecting payments and making change? It wouldn't hurt the older woman to take orders and serve customers for the time being.

As Juliet walked away, she massaged the small of her back with both hands.

Damn. It grated on Mark to see her working so hard. And hurting.

But hey, he reminded himself. That really wasn't any of his business. He ought to be relieved that she hadn't waited on him this evening. That she hadn't made any effort to stop by his table—in spite of the friendly conversation they'd shared last night.

Yet the fact that she hadn't come by bothered him, too.

He missed her smile, her wit. Her company.

But then why wouldn't he? Juliet was about the only person, place or thing in this town he found interesting or appealing.

And she hadn't looked his way this evening.

Was she avoiding him? Had he been too intrusive last night? Offering his opinion and advice without being asked?

Maybe so, but that was just as well.

Last night, following their chat, he'd gone back to

the Wander-On Inn and, when he'd finally dozed off, he'd slept like hell, tossing and turning all night long like a trout trapped in shallow water.

He glanced up from the trace of meat loaf and mashed potatoes on his plate and saw her coming his way.

Well, what do you know? Speak of the pretty devil who'd triggered his insomnia.

When she reached his table, she smiled. "Mary Sue had to go home because of a family emergency. So I'm going to be taking care of you from here on out."

"You're the one who should be cutting out early. And someone ought to be taking care of *you*."

She arched, grimaced, then rubbed her lower back. "We've already talked about that."

They had. And he hadn't meant to get her all riled up. After all, it wasn't his place to harp on her. And even if she appreciated his concern, he wouldn't be around long enough to nurture a friendship. Besides, he damn sure didn't need to get involved with a single mother and her child, especially when they lived in a town he'd been avoiding for twenty years.

"I'm sorry, Juliet. I'll let it go."

"Thanks." She offered him an olive-branch smile. "I'm trying to take it easy, Mark. But I've got to keep working a little while longer."

He nodded. She was concerned about finances, which was understandable. Once she gave birth and went back to work, the cost of a babysitter would probably put a crunch on her paycheck.

Maybe he ought to give her some money. Five hundred dollars might make life a bit easier for her. And then he could let it go. Ease off. Let her be.

"Can I get you some dessert?" she asked. "Buck made his blue-ribbon peach cobbler today. And everyone's been raving about it."

"Sure. I'll take some." Mark placed his napkin on the table and pushed aside his dinner plate. "Will you join me?"

"Maybe for a minute." She glanced over her shoulder at Martha, who appeared preoccupied with sorting bills in the cash drawer. "I've had a nagging backache all afternoon."

Mark couldn't hold back a grumble. If he were a violent man, he'd slam a fist on the table in frustration. Was a backache normal for a woman in her condition? Or was it an indication that something was wrong? Something terribly wrong? Something that put her life and that of her baby at risk?

Like Kelly.

Damn the memory that wouldn't let him alone.

No matter what he'd told himself, no matter what kind of truce he and the waitress had drawn, Mark couldn't shake his concern. "I'm glad you're going to take a break, but come on, Juliet. You really need to go home and put your feet up. Think about the baby."

"I am." Her eyes locked on his in rebuttal, although they appeared a bit glassy, like they were swimming in emotion and barely staying afloat. "I don't have a family to fall back on. It's just the baby and me. And I can't help worrying about making ends meet, about keeping a roof over our heads once he or she gets here."

"Yeah, well unless you want that baby to get here too soon, you'd better heed the doctor's advice and quit work."

"Tonight, when I clock out, I'll ask for a couple of days off. Okay?" She lifted a delicate brow, as though cueing him to agree.

He merely blew out a sigh, giving in—so it appeared. He didn't usually offer unsolicited advice. It wasn't normally his style. But then again, he wasn't reminded of Kelly that often. Of her unnecessary death.

Juliet seemed to accept his silence as acquiescence, which it was. But her weary smile didn't take the edge off the exhaustion in her expression. Nor did it erase the dark circles he hadn't noticed under her eyes last night.

"I'll have two peach cobblers," he said. "And a glass of milk."

"I'd think the milk might curdle in your stomach with the bourbon you drank earlier."

"The milk is for you."

She nodded, then went after the dessert. When she returned, she took a seat. "How's your story coming along?"

"What story? This assignment is a joke." And it was, compared to the bigger stories he'd covered in the past. Important events that made him feel as though he'd reached the professional level he'd strived for, that level where one man—a reporter—could make a difference in people's lives.

"You think the gold rush is a joke?" she asked.

"Writing a story about a bunch of loony-tune prospectors who've flocked to a possible gold rush in Thunder Canyon can't even come close to a story about a major flood or fire." He dug into the cobbler and scooped out a gooey bite. Hmmm. Not bad.

When he glanced up, he caught Juliet's eye, her rapt attention.

"You'd rather write about disasters?" she asked. "Why such depressing news?"

"It touches hearts, confronts our deepest fears. Stirs up emotion."

"We had a fight in here last Saturday night. There was plenty of emotion stirring then." Her lips quirked into a grin, and he realized she was teasing him, trying to chip away at the cynical armor it had taken him years to build.

"A fight, huh? I'm sorry I missed the entertainment. But not to worry. I can go down to the E.R. at Thunder Canyon General and watch them stitch up the scalp of some idiot who tripped over a pickax and split his head open."

"So this is small tomatoes for you."

"Small potatoes," he corrected, unwilling to reveal his disappointment, his frustration. His desire to make a difference, to help people—victims of disasters. And to better prepare people who hadn't been stricken by major calamities yet. He shrugged. "I'll get the job done."

"You know," she said, licking a dollop of peach cobbler from her fork. "There have been some gold nuggets found. So one of the prospectors *could* strike it rich."

"Maybe. But I think the biggest story I've got is the hullabaloo about the ownership of the old mine."

"I thought Caleb Douglas owned it. That his great-grandfather won it in a poker game with the Shady Lady."

"That's the legend that's been circulating for years. People have just assumed that Caleb was the owner. But he hasn't produced the deed."

She furrowed her brow. "What about the county records?"

"They're not available right now. Harvey Watson, the clerk who's been transcribing all the old records into the new computer system, is on vacation." Mark slowly shook his head. "Can you believe, in this day and age, that Thunder Canyon would be so far behind the times?"

"Like I told you before, I think this historical old town is quaint."

He leaned back in his chair, watched the innocence dance in her eyes and smiled. "You must have some Amish in your genes."

"Sorry, no Amish. Just a little Basque, a drop or two of French. But mostly, a healthy blend of proud Mexican and Old World Spanish." She smiled and gave a little wink. "Maybe I was born in the wrong century."

She was definitely unique. A novelty. And as far as he was concerned, her bloodlines were damn near perfect.

"So, who do you think owns the Queen of Hearts

mine?" she asked. "You ought to have an idea. After all, you're a local boy."

Not *that* local. Mark hadn't moved to Thunder Canyon until he was thirteen. And he was long gone five years later. "I think Caleb Douglas owns the property, and it's just a matter of a misplaced deed and some backward record keeping in a land office. Anyway, that's my guess."

She took a sip of milk, and he watched the path of her swallow. She had a pretty neck. Regal and aristocratic. The kind of throat and neck a man liked to nuzzle.

When she lowered the glass, she wore a spot of white at the edge of her mouth. Unable to help himself, he reached out and snagged it with his thumb.

Her lips parted, and something—he sure as hell didn't know what—passed between them. An awareness. An intimacy. Something he hadn't bargained for.

"I…umm…I'm sorry. You had a little milk…" He pointed to her cheek.

Juliet swiped her fingers across her mouth, trying to remove any trace of milk that still lingered. Or maybe she was trying to prolong the stimulating warmth of Mark's touch. The flutter of heat his thumb had provoked.

For goodness' sake. She was acting like a schoolgirl with a crush on the substitute teacher, a handsome young man fresh out of college and thrown into a classroom of adolescents. Or on a guy who was way out of her league. And that was crazy.

With the healthy sense of pride Papa and *Abuelita* had instilled in her, there weren't too many people—or men—Juliet would consider above her reach.

Of course, being nearly eight months pregnant certainly left her out of the running when it came to romance.

She glanced across the room, eager to break eye contact, or whatever was buzzing between her and Mark, and spotted Mrs. Tasker sitting in the swivel seat at the register. The older woman wore a frown that made the wrinkles around her eyes more pronounced.

Were her ingrown nails giving her trouble again tonight? Or did she think Juliet had a crush on the handsome older man, that she was trying to strike up a relationship with a customer?

Maybe she was thinking Juliet ought to get back to work.

"Oh, for Pete's sake," Mark said. "Tell Attila the Hun to back off and let you have a decent break."

He was right—not about Mrs. Tasker being a barbarian, but about Juliet needing to quit for today. This darn backache was getting to her. "I'll take the rest of the night off, all right?"

"That's better yet." He caught her fingers in a gentle squeeze before releasing them. But the brief connection remained, humming between them as though he hadn't let go.

She shook it off, blaming her hormones and the loneliness that seemed to haunt her at times, ever since her brother's accident.

It had been two years, although time had eased the

pain and dulled the shock, as Father Tomas had told her it would. But time hadn't done a darn thing to ease the loneliness or to change the fact she didn't have a family anymore.

She brushed a hand along the contour of her tummy, caressed the knot that sprung up on the left side. A little foot? A knee? A fist?

As she stood, the muscles of her back gripped hard, causing her to bend and grab the table for support.

"What's the matter?" Mark jumped to his feet.

"I'm not sure."

For a woman with bad feet, Mrs. Tasker was by her side in an instant. "Are you in labor?"

Juliet froze as the possibility momentarily hovered over her like the calm before the storm. "No, I don't think so." At least, she hoped not. It was still too early.

As the ache in her back continued, she closed her eyes. *Dios, por favor.* Don't let it happen now. It's too soon.

"Are you having a contraction?" Mrs. Tasker asked, glancing at her wristwatch, as though she meant to start timing the pains.

"It's just a backache," Juliet said, willing it to be true.

The older woman crossed her arms in an all-knowing fashion. "That's how my labor started with Jimmy. All in my back."

Juliet lifted her gaze, looked at Mark, expecting him to blurt out a gripe, a complaint, an I-told-you-so. But the only sign of his response was a tense jaw, a pale face.

"No need for us to take any chances," Mrs. Tasker said. "I'll call an ambulance."

"Don't bother." Mark reached into his back pocket, took out his wallet, withdrew a twenty-dollar bill and dropped it on the table. "I'll take her to the hospital."

Juliet began to object, to tell him to finish his dessert. But he slipped an arm around her and led her to the front door.

Mark followed White Water Drive to Thunder Canyon General, then veered toward the separate emergency entrance. He stopped under the covered portico, close to the automatic glass doors, and threw the car into park. "Wait here."

Leaving Juliet in the idling car, he dashed inside past a security guard, his heart pounding as though he had a personal stake in this—and he sure as hell didn't.

But Mark knew firsthand how things could go wrong during labor. And he wasn't going to leave Juliet, who didn't have anyone to depend on, to fend for herself. Neither was he going to let her ignore any symptoms that might be serious.

He spotted a nurse behind the reception desk. "I need help. Now. I've got a woman in my car who may be in premature labor."

The nurse grabbed a wheelchair and followed him outside. But rather than take Juliet right to a room, she stopped at the reception desk.

"Can't this wait?" Mark asked, growing more agitated by the second. He wanted to hand over Juliet to a qualified professional, then get the heck out of here.

"I'm sorry," the nurse responded. "This will only take a minute."

She was wrong. But while the customary paperwork was filled out, Mark managed to not pitch a fit about the amount of time it took.

Finally, Juliet was given a temporary bed in the E.R. Her only privacy was a blue-and-white striped curtain that didn't reach the floor.

Before long, she'd had her temperature and blood pressure taken—all within normal range.

Mark really ought to loosen up. Normal was a good thing, right?

"Did you notify your physician that you were coming in?" the nurse asked Juliet.

"I didn't have time to think about it." Juliet glanced at Mark and blew out a sigh. "Can you tell Dr. Emerson that I'm here?"

The nurse, a matronly blonde, placed a hand on Juliet's shoulder. "Dr. Emerson had a heart attack last night and is in ICU."

Juliet gasped.

"But don't you worry," the nurse said. "We have a top-notch resident obstetrician who will take good care of you."

"Dr. Hart?" Juliet asked.

The nurse smiled. "That's right."

"I saw her on Sunday afternoon. I'd had a fainting spell. And you're right. I felt very comfortable with her."

"Good," the nurse said. "I'll give Dr. Hart a call and see whether she'd like us to examine you down here or send you to maternity on the second floor."

Juliet uttered an okay. She might be comfortable with the resident obstetrician, but Mark could see the worry in her eyes. The anxiety in her face.

"In the meantime," the nurse said, pointing to a chair beside the bed. "Why don't you have a seat, Dad?"

Dad? She had that all wrong. But before Mark could explain, Juliet did it for him. "This is my friend, Mark Anderson. He's not the baby's father."

The nurse smiled. "It's nice for a woman to have someone she trusts be her birth coach."

Birth coach? Whoa. Not Mark. He'd just brought Juliet here to make sure she saw a doctor, that she was someplace safe. Maybe he could stick around and hold her hand for a while. But if things got hairy, if she was really in labor, he'd wait in the cafeteria until she gave birth. Heck, he might even hang around long enough to look at the baby behind a glass window and tell her the kid was cute—even though he'd seen a couple of newborns and thought they looked more like aliens than humans.

Then, after that, he'd be on his way.

When the nurse stepped out, Mark took a seat, but he couldn't seem to relax. What was taking so long? He glanced at his watch. The minute hands seemed to be moving slower than usual.

A while later—he didn't know how long—another nurse arrived. A friendly, thirty-something woman with short, dark-hair and wearing a pink smock dotted with teddy bears. "Ms. Rivera? I'm Beth Ann. Dr. Hart has asked me to take you to maternity."

The nurse fiddled with the bed, making it mobile, then began to push Juliet out of the E.R. and into the hall. She slowed her steps just long enough to glance at Mark. "You can follow us."

He opened his mouth to object, to say he'd be having coffee in the cafeteria, but for some reason, he fell into step behind the rolling bed.

They took an elevator to the second floor, then the nurse wheeled Juliet toward the maternity ward, where she paused before the ominous double doors.

Mark's steps slowed, too. But not because he was tagging along behind them.

What the hell was he doing? Juliet was in good hands. Competent hands. He didn't need to go in there. They didn't need *him*. Besides, he'd done his duty. His good deed for the day.

But when Juliet turned her head and looked at him, those misty, mahogany eyes locking on his, he saw the fear, the nervousness. The need.

He offered her a wimpy smile, and when she turned her head away, he ran a hand through his hair. He didn't have any business going in there with her. He wasn't the baby's father. Or her husband.

But Juliet didn't have a mother or a sister. She was new in town. And he doubted she'd made any friends, not with her schedule. Hell, none of her co-workers had jumped in to help.

Right now, she only had him.

The nurse pressed at the button that automatically swung open the doors, then pushed Juliet through.

Mark followed behind, like a clueless steer on its way to a slaughterhouse.

They plodded along the hall, his Italian loafers clicking on the spanking clean floor, the nurse's rubber soles making a dull squeak with each step. They passed several open doorways Mark was afraid to peek into and continued along a glass-enclosed room that held incubators for the tiniest and sickest of patients. All of the little beds were empty, thank God.

Would Juliet's baby be placed in one of them?

The possibility jolted his heart, jump-starting his pulse.

Oh, for cripes sake. Mark wasn't a worrier. Not by nature. It was just the pregnancy, the vulnerability of both woman and child.

And his own fears brought back to life.

He swore under his breath. Juliet was just having a backache, right? From working too hard and carrying the extra weight of a baby. She hadn't been especially worried until Martha Tasker popped up like a jack-in-the-box, with the tale of her own labor, stirring things up. Making something out of nothing.

Mark followed the bed into a room that looked more like a bedroom than a private hospital room. Pale green curtains graced the window that looked out into a frozen courtyard that was probably colorful and vibrant during the summer.

Decorated in pink, green and a touch of lavender, the color scheme and homey touch of the room probably helped ease the nerves of laboring expectant mothers. But it didn't do a damn thing to ease Mark's anxiety, not when he spotted medical gaskets and giz-mos that reminded him of where they were, what they faced.

"Here's a gown," Beth Ann said. "As soon as you slip it on, I'll examine you."

An examination? Oh, cripes. Not an internal exam.

The nurse asked Juliet, "Would you like him to stay in here?"

Oh, hell no. Not on a bet. Mark cleared his throat, then started backing toward the door. "Why don't I step out of the room for a little while. You can come and get me when it's all over."

When it was *all* over. Not just the exam.

The nurse nodded as she reached for a box of rub-ber gloves.

Mark couldn't get out of the birthing room fast enough. If he ever had a kid of his own, he wouldn't be hanging around and watching that kind of a pro-cedure. No way.

He ran a finger under the collar of his shirt, then scanned the hospital corridor, where a floral wallpa-per border softened the sterile white walls.

If there'd been anyone else who could be here for Juliet, he'd be out of here faster than a sopping-wet dog could shake its fur.

But she didn't have anyone.

And that's why he stayed.

Moments later, the nurse poked her head out the door. "You can come in now."

He nodded, then stepped inside. But before he reached Juliet's bed, an attractive woman dressed in medical garb approached and introduced herself as Dr. Hart.

"I think she's in the early stages of labor," the nurse told the obstetrician. "And she's about two centimeters dilated."

Dr. Hart nodded, then approached Juliet. "I'd feel better about delivering your baby a couple weeks from now. So I'd like to give you something to stop labor and another medication that will help the baby's lungs develop quicker, in case your labor doesn't respond to treatment."

When the doctor and nurse left them alone, Juliet shot Mark a wobbly grin. "You don't have to stick around. I'll be okay."

Hey, there was his out. His excuse to leave. But he couldn't take it, couldn't walk away knowing she was all alone. "What if you need a ride home?"

"I can take a cab."

"Don't be ridiculous." Then he sat back in his chair, unsure of what the night would bring.

And hoping to hell he could step up to the plate.

This time.

Chapter Three

Juliet stretched out in the hospital bed, wishing she could go back to sleep. The medication Dr. Hart had given her last night seemed to have worked. The back-ache had eased completely within the first hour of her arrival.

But that didn't mean she'd rested well. And neither had Mark, who'd stayed by her side the entire night.

More than once she'd told him he could go back to the inn, but he'd refused. And she had to admit, she was glad he hadn't left her alone.

She suspected hanging out with a pregnant woman at the hospital hadn't been easy for him. A couple of times, he'd gotten a squeamish I'd-rather-be-any-where-but-here look on his face. But he'd persevered like a real trooper.

Now he dozed on a pale green recliner near the window, hands folded over the flat plain of his stomach, eyes closed, dark hair spiked and mussed. He lay there for a while, unaware of her interest. And then he stirred.

She watched him arch his back, twist, extend his arms, then cover a yawn with his fist. When his eyes opened, he caught her gaze. "Good morning. How are you feeling?"

"Tired, but the backache is gone."

"That's good news." He gripped the armrests, manipulating the chair to an upright position, and stood like a knight in rumpled armor.

And that's how she thought of him. Real hero material—in the rough.

With a wrinkled cotton dress shirt and tousled hair, the cynical reporter might not make another woman sit up and take notice this morning. But another woman hadn't appreciated him pinch-hitting for the men she no longer had in her life.

Her brother Manny had been a macho guy, tough and gruff on the outside. But he'd also been a softy in the middle—at least, when it came to his little sister. And Mark appeared to be cut from the same bolt of cloth—a comparison made without any effort on her part.

There were men, as Juliet had learned the hard way, who wouldn't stand by a pregnant woman.

Her baby's father was one of them.

For a moment, as Juliet watched a sturdy, broad-shouldered Mark walk toward the window, she pretended that she had someone in her corner. Someone who cared enough to stick by her.

And, at least for the past twelve hours, that had been true. Mark had been there for her when she needed a friend. And that was something she'd remember long after he'd taken another assignment and left Thunder Canyon.

She watched as he drew the floral curtains aside, allowing her to peer into the dawn-lit hospital courtyard. She wondered what the grounds looked like in the summer, when the patches of snow had all melted and the rose garden bloomed.

The door to the birthing room cracked open, and they both turned as Dr. Hart entered. The slender woman with light brown, shoulder-length hair approached the bed. As in the past, she exuded professionalism and concern. Yet last night Juliet had noticed something different about her. A happy glow that lingered this morning.

"Good morning," the doctor said. "Did you have a restful night?"

"I didn't sleep too well," Juliet admitted, "but I'm feeling all right. No apparent labor."

"Let's make sure there hasn't been any silent dilation going on," the doctor said, as she headed for the sink.

As before, Mark left the room to give her privacy.

After washing her hands, Dr. Hart donned a pair of gloves and nodded toward the closed door. "That's some friend you have."

"It looks that way." Juliet closed her eyes during the

exam, whispering a prayer that all was well. That she hadn't dilated any more, that her baby was safe in her womb for the time being.

"Good," Dr. Hart said, removing the gloves and tossing them in the trash. "Nothing's changed since last night."

Juliet blew out the breath she'd been holding, as Dr. Hart opened the door to call Mark back into the room.

"I think we're home free," the obstetrician told him. "This time."

"Thank goodness." Mark blew out a little whistle and slid Juliet a smile, providing a sense of camaraderie. Teamwork. Something she hadn't experienced since her brother's accident.

The doctor made a note in the chart, then glanced at Juliet. "If you promise to stay off your feet, I'll let you go home."

"That's great." Juliet knew she'd feel better in the privacy of her own little apartment, close to her photographs and memories. "Thank you."

"But I'm talking extreme bed rest," the doctor stressed.

Mark cleared his throat. "Juliet doesn't have anyone to look after her, so maybe she ought to stay here."

For several weeks? Was he crazy? "That's ridiculous, Mark. I'll rest better and be happier at home."

Dr. Hart glanced up from the chart. "I'm not sure how your insurance carrier will feel about you staying here for more than a day or so. Do you have someone who can stay with you?"

"No, I live alone. But I promise to take it easy."

"Oh, yeah?" Mark made his way to Juliet's bed-side. He'd seen the way she'd been "taking it easy" at The Hitching Post. "Doctor, you can't trust her not to get up and do the dishes or scrub floors or clean out closets or something like that."

"Then maybe we'd better keep you here." Dr. Hart, attractive even in green hospital scrubs, leaned her hip against the bed and crossed her arms.

Disappointment swept over Juliet's face, and Mark felt like a real spoilsport. But she didn't have anyone to look after her. He doubted Mrs. Tasker, who liked to park her butt by the cash register, would volunteer to help.

Juliet looked at him and frowned, tossing a guilt trip on him.

Mark supposed *he* could check on her. After all he was staying across the street.

"I can look after her." The comment popped out before Mark could think about the ramifications. And when Juliet and the doctor faced him, he realized backpedaling would be next to impossible now. He was committed. And he'd taken a stand. But that didn't mean his gut wasn't twisting.

Juliet shot him a wide-eyed stare. "You can't be se-rious about staying with me."

"Why not?" The question couldn't have surprised her any more than it had him. Hell, Mark had not only volunteered to babysit a woman who was on the verge of going into labor, but now he was trying to convince her—and maybe even himself—that it was a good idea.

"You can't waste your time taking care of me." Juliet pressed the control button that raised her up in bed. "You've got work to do."

He shook his head. "I don't have anything pressing to do."

"That's not true," she countered. "You've got a news article to write."

"The story, as I've told you before, is a joke. And the article can practically write itself."

"So, what's the verdict," Dr. Hart asked. "Do I sign these release papers or not?"

Mark crossed his arms. "Sign them."

"All right," the doctor said. "I'll have the paperwork processed. Then I'll send an orderly to take you out in a wheelchair."

When Dr. Hart left the room, Mark ran a hand through his hair. Juliet's back might feel much better this morning, but his hurt like hell.

What he really needed to do was get out of here, shower and maybe take a nap.

He glanced at Juliet and saw reluctance in her expression. Resentment, too? He wasn't sure. But she'd been overruled, and he had a feeling it didn't sit well.

Strangely, for a guy who liked to come out on top himself, he wasn't feeling too happy about winning this argument.

And he hoped to hell he hadn't bitten off more than he could chew.

Thirty minutes later, Mark brought his rental car to the curb at the main entrance of the hospital. Then he helped Juliet into the passenger seat.

He was taking her home. And that fact brought on a flurry of other concerns, things he hadn't considered when he'd volunteered to look after her.

There was no way around it. He would have to put in a significant amount of time with her. He'd told the doctor he'd take care of her, not pop in and out several times a day.

What if something went wrong in the middle of the night?

He'd have to stay there until she was no longer at risk for premature labor.

But how big was her place?

Where would he sleep?

On the sofa, he supposed.

The crick in his back, the one he'd woken up with, ached all the more, just thinking about being camped on her sofa for the next week or so. Damn. He was going to have to see a chiropractor when this stint in Thunder Canyon was over.

As they drove past the newly constructed Ranch View Estates, Juliet peered out the window, studying the pine tree-lined entrance, the bright, colorful flags and a sign announcing that Phase I was now available.

"That's a nice housing development," she said. "One afternoon, on my day off, I looked at the models."

Mark nodded, but didn't comment. He didn't have any inclination to set down roots, to purchase a home and landscape a yard. Especially not in Thunder Canyon.

At thirty-eight, he'd yet to buy a place of his own.

And why should he? He was always off on assignment, living in hotels that the news service paid for.

He turned left onto Main and followed it until they neared The Hitching Post.

"Can you drive around to the rear entrance?" Juliet asked. "I don't feel like going through the dining room looking like this."

"Sure." He didn't think she looked bad at all, not after what she'd been through. But he didn't argue. He swung around to the back, where a black Chevy S-10 pickup with a vinyl cover on the bed was parked next to a trash bin.

Mark nodded toward the custom truck with a lowered chassis. "Whose is that?"

"It's mine."

"You drive a pickup?" He chuckled. The lady was full of surprises. "Somehow, I figured you would drive a racy red sports car or a flashy white convertible."

"Hey, that little truck is special to me. It was my brother's pride and joy."

Was?

She'd told him the baby was her only family.

Unable to quell his curiosity, he asked, "What happened to him?"

"He died about eighteen months ago, and since he'd listed me on the title, I inherited his truck."

"I'm sorry," Mark said, the words feeling inadequate but necessary.

"I'm sorry, too."

A heavy silence filled the interior of the car, and Mark wanted it to end, wanted to lighten the mood.

To make her feel better. But it was hard to know what to say to someone who'd lost a loved one. He knew how impotent sympathetic words could be. No one had been able to ease his grief after his sister died. Not when her death had been his fault.

His parents had never forgiven him for what had happened that stormy evening. But he supposed that was to be expected. He'd never forgiven himself, either.

"It's tough not having a family," Juliet said, breaking the stifling stillness that had nearly choked the air out of the sedan. "But I focus on the memories we had. It's what Father Tomas, our parish priest, advised me to do. And it helps."

Mark was glad she had memories to rely on. He didn't. At least not the kind that made him feel better. In a way, he'd lost his entire family, too, even though his parents were still alive and kicking.

When his mom had learned he was in town, she'd called him at the Wander-On Inn. She'd sounded hurt that he hadn't chosen to stay at the motel she and his dad had owned and operated for the past twenty-five years.

Mark had told her it was because the company had prepaid his room without knowing his family could provide him free lodging. But to be honest, Mark had been very specific with the company's travel agent when they'd talked about where he wanted to stay— *anywhere but The Big Sky Motel at the edge of town.*

After parking beside Juliet's pickup, he spotted the stairway that led to the second floor.

He supposed he shouldn't be surprised that The Hitching Post didn't have an elevator, not when the county land office was just beginning to convert their records to a computer system. He bit back a swear word, but couldn't stop the grumble that slipped out.

"What's the matter?" she asked.

"I'm going to have to get you upstairs."

She opened her mouth, as if to object, then closed it again. Apparently, the recent bout of premature labor had made her realize how vulnerable she was.

He slid out of the driver's seat, circled the car and opened her door, intent upon carrying her.

She put her hand up to stop him. "Maybe if I take the steps really slow—"

He shook his head. "No way. Climbing stairs isn't a good idea. It's too strenuous."

"I can't let you carry me." She glanced down at her belly and frowned. "I'm too heavy."

She might be pregnant, but she was a petite woman. Small boned.

"Don't be silly. You're a lightweight."

"Open your eyes, Mark." She stroked her stomach.

Heck. Women could be so testy about their weight— even when they weren't pregnant. As he opened his mouth to argue, he caught a glimpse of skepticism in her frown.

Hey, wait a minute. Was she doubting his ability to carry her?

His male pride bristled. "Listen, sweetheart. I'm probably ten to fifteen years older than you, but that doesn't make me over the hill yet."

She balked momentarily, as though contemplating a fight, but she slipped an arm through the shoulder strap of her purse, swung her legs over the side of the seat, draped a hand around his neck and let him scoop her up.

She was heavier than he'd expected, but she was all belly. How big was the kid?

As he lifted her from the rented sedan, he choked back any sound she might consider a winded effort. But once he'd straightened and kicked the passenger door shut, it wasn't so bad. In fact, he kind of liked holding her in his arms and feeling like some kind of kick-ass hero.

Her arm looped around his neck. Holding on. Holding him.

He carried her up the steps, nails in the wood creaking under their combined weight. Damn, he hoped that whoever had built this stairway had made it sturdy. And that it hadn't been the original staircase. No telling what more than a hundred years of wear and tear had done to the structure.

"Mark, wait. I'm really uneasy. That can't be good for the baby, either."

She was right. He let her down, then helped her walk the rest of the way. Slowly. Carefully. Step by step.

When they reached the top landing, she dug through her purse for the key, but instead of unlocking the door, she turned to him instead. Her belly brushed against him, tempting him to touch it. To see what it felt like. But he refrained.

Her eyes sparked with sincerity. "I can stay alone. Really. Maybe, if I give you a key, you can stop in and check on me several times a day."

The idea had merit. But Mark had promised the doctor he'd look after her. And that's what he intended to do. "If it's okay, I can stay with you. Besides, I'm stuck in town anyway—at least until the county clerk returns and I can have a look at those old recorded deeds."

Her eyes widened and her lips parted. "Are you going to move into my place?"

No. He couldn't do that. Ever since his wife had left him and filed for divorce—way back when— Mark had learned to protect himself, his freedom. His secrets.

Even when he was seriously dating someone, he'd maintained a distance. He didn't like the idea of having his toothbrush and razor claim space on someone else's bathroom counter or on a shelf inside a medicine cabinet. Unless, of course, it was in a hotel room on a lover's getaway weekend.

But this was different.

Still, he couldn't bring himself to check out of the inn completely. It wasn't a matter of saving money. It was saving his space. His privacy. His ability to slip away before things got complicated.

"No, I'm keeping the room at the inn." As an explanation, he added, "With all the fortune hunters who've clamored into town, rooms are limited. And if I give up my place across the street, I might not be able to find another one."

And that was true. Mark sure as hell wouldn't ask his folks if he could stay with them. Not at the small mountaintop home they owned. Not even on a couch in the office of The Big Sky Motel.

"If you'll be okay for a while," he said, "I'll go across the street and bring over a few personal items. A change of clothes."

She flashed him a battle-weary but confident smile. "I'll be fine. Remember, I'm the one who wanted to stay alone."

He nodded, waiting as she turned her back and slipped the key in the lock. After she opened the door, he followed her inside.

The scent of cleaning products mingled with a hint of paint, as he entered a living room that didn't have any walls separating it from the kitchen or dining area. He glanced around, eyes adjusting to the darkened interior.

She flipped on a switch, turning on a goofy wagon wheel chandelier that lit the room, revealing a brown tweed sofa, a black recliner and a maple coffee table.

A trace of old cigarette smoke that a good scrubbing and a paint job hadn't been able to hide lingered in the gold drapes and the green shag carpet.

"Why don't you lie down," he said. "I'll be right back."

As he turned to go, she grabbed the sleeve of his shirt, those rich mahogany eyes snaring his, setting his nerves on edge, making his heart rumble in his chest.

"Thanks…for…you know…" She gave a little shrug. "For everything."

"No problem." But as he stepped into the crisp, cool morning air, he wasn't so sure he'd done anything commendable.

Juliet wasn't in a hospital—where she belonged.

And Mark, who had volunteered to be her private duty nurse, didn't know squat about pregnant women, childbirth or babies.

What in the hell had he set himself up for?

Juliet stretched out on the sofa, her head propped up on two pillows. As she thumbed through a *Parents* magazine, a knock sounded at the door.

She glanced up from an article on breast-feeding that had caught her eye. "Mark?"

"Yeah. It's me."

"The door is unlocked. Come on in." She fingered the fringed lapel of her blue robe, hoping he wouldn't give her a hard time because she'd taken a shower and shampooed her hair. But she'd been careful and had taken it slow and easy.

Mark, who looked shower-fresh himself, strode into the room with a newspaper tucked under his arm and carrying a gray duffel bag in his hand. His gaze zoomed in on her, and he frowned. "Why is your hair wet?"

"I took a quick shower. No strain, no stress."

"I don't think that's what the doctor meant by extreme bed rest."

"Maybe not, but I'll rest easier if I'm clean."

He scanned the interior of her apartment, as though noting the Early-American-Garage-Sale decor, the mismatched furniture, the decoupage wall plaques that served as artwork.

So the apartment was a little drab. She was happy here. She lifted her chin, prepared to defend her home from a remark that didn't come.

He nodded toward the wagon wheel chandelier that hung over the dinette table. "Those are low-watt bulbs. Do you mind if we have some more light in here?"

"No, go ahead."

She expected him to turn on another lamp, but he strode toward the window and paused in front of the ugly gold drapes.

The droopy, rundown condition wasn't her fault. And there wasn't anything she could do about it. The rod was missing some of those little plastic thingies the metal hooks poked into.

But, hey. As long as she had privacy, she could live with them. After all, she'd lived with worse and been happy. When love and laughter filled the interior of a home, nothing else mattered.

He glanced over his shoulder. "You need to ask your landlord to replace the curtains."

"I'm not going to push for anything like that right now. Not when Mrs. Tasker is going to be shorthanded in the diner and might have to replace me."

He started to say something, but turned toward the curtain rod. He fiddled with the cord until he opened the drapes a couple of feet.

"I rented this place furnished," she told him. "So I can't be too fussy."

Again, he withheld a comment, although she

wished he hadn't. She was prepared to argue. There was no need for him to feel sorry for her. She was glad to be in Thunder Canyon. Glad to have a job and a home for her baby. There was a lot to be said for counting one's blessings.

She reached for the soft green *covijita* that draped over the back of the old sofa and pulled it close, brushing it against her cheek. Her *abuelita* had crocheted the small blanket, and Juliet cherished it.

"How many bedrooms do you have?" Mark glanced at the two doors along the east wall.

"Just one. The bathroom is on the left. The other door is the bedroom. Go ahead and put your bag in there. I'll take the sofa."

"No way." He crossed his arms, standing sentry-straight, brow furrowed as though she'd suggested they run naked in a snowstorm.

"Shall we compromise?" She figured they could share turns.

"Sure. You take the sofa by day, and I'll take it by night."

She could argue, but what was the use? Mark was only looking out for her best interests. Besides, there would probably be plenty of times in upcoming days when they'd disagree. It was best if she chose her battles with this man.

Mark moved toward the bookcase where Juliet displayed her family photos instead of books. Her father had built it years ago. As far as quality, the wood was rustic and slightly flawed, but the piece of furniture was priceless.

He lifted a silver framed photograph of *Abuelita* holding Papa when he was a toddler.

"Did these pictures come with the place?" he asked.

"No. That's my father when he was just a little boy. And that's his mother. My *abuelita*."

He replaced it and chose the one of Manny in his baseball uniform.

"That's my brother, Manuel. He loved sports."

Mark studied the photo for a while. "What kind of accident did he have?"

"It happened at the warehouse where he worked. A freak industrial accident, they told me. Involving a forklift." She laid the magazine across her lap and tried to focus on something more pleasant. Something that didn't remind her of her brother's death, the lawsuit. Something that didn't trigger thoughts of Erik Kramer, the attorney who'd volunteered to handle her interests in the workman's compensation case. The jerk.

Mark replaced the silver frame, then turned away from the shelves. "I'm sorry your family isn't around for you now."

She shrugged and mustered a smile. "I have a lot of happy memories. Of the good times. And the unconditional love." She ran a hand along the contour of her tummy, caressing her child. "And I have a new baby to look forward to. Life goes on."

He merely studied her, looking skeptical. Hopeful. Concerned. A hodgepodge of emotion she found hard to decipher played havoc with his expression. But it didn't do a thing to lessen the attraction that continued to build—in spite of her circumstances.

Dios mio, the man was handsome. Or maybe she found him more appealing, now that she'd gotten to know him better.

It felt weird to have him here. But at the same time, it was kind of nice. And she found it hard not to stare.

He slipped off his black leather jacket, hung it over the back of the recliner and sauntered toward the sofa. He'd dressed casually today, sporting a pair of worn jeans and a long-sleeved chambray shirt.

As he drew close, she caught a whiff of mountain-fresh cologne, menthol shaving cream and peppermint toothpaste. It was a taunting scent. Mesmerizing in a way. Her gaze locked on his, her pulse kicking up a notch. Did he know? Could he sense her inappropriate interest?

He cleared his throat. "It's nearly nine o'clock, so we'd better think about breakfast."

The husky sound of his voice, more graveled than usual, made her wonder if he'd ever been a smoker. If so, he'd given up the habit.

"You've got to be hungry," he added.

She was. But she hadn't realized it until now.

"Can I get you anything?"

"I'll have a glass of milk. For the baby."

He walked to the kitchen, opened the fridge and pulled out a carton of milk. Then he rummaged through the cupboards, looking for a glass. She could have helped him out, she supposed, telling him where to look, but she watched him instead, her interest and curiosity piqued. There was something about a man in the kitchen. Especially that man.

There was so much she didn't know about Mark, other than he was a reporter who'd once been a local boy.

"Do you still have family around here?" she asked.

His movements slowed. "Yeah. My parents."

That was nice. "Do you see them often?"

"No." He filled the glass until the milk frothed at the top. "My folks and I had a falling out years ago."

"That's too bad."

He shrugged. "We were never that close anyway."

"Have you tried a reconciliation?" She knew the value of a family, the value of turning the other cheek. Of appreciating each individual personality, in spite of the differences. And the value of appreciating what you had, while you still had it.

"We talk, if that's what you mean. But we aren't very close. And I like it that way." He brought her the milk. "Do you have anything I can use to make breakfast?"

He was going to cook? By himself?

Her father and brother couldn't have fixed themselves a meal—maybe because *Abuelita* had claimed the kitchen as her territory. And even after she passed away, they hadn't stepped foot near the stove. So, at the age of ten, Juliet had taken over. And eventually she became a pretty decent cook.

"I have eggs and bacon in the fridge," she told him. "Orange juice, too. And the coffee is in the small canister on the counter."

"Okay. I'll fix something for us to eat. You just rest."

Actually, she thought watching Sir Rumpled Knight in the kitchen might prove to be entertaining.

And touching.

If she let herself dream, she could imagine falling for a guy like Mark. But Juliet knew better than to let any romantic, fairy-tale notions take root. Her heart had already borne more than its share of grief, and there was no need to set herself up for a fall that was easy to foresee.

Besides, Juliet came from sturdy stock. She was a survivor. And she didn't need to be rescued, didn't need anyone to look after her once the baby got here.

Especially not a globe-trotting reporter who'd made it clear that he was just passing through.

She returned her attention to the magazine she'd been reading, to the article on breast-feeding dos and don'ts.

And she remained focused on the words—until she caught a whiff of burning bacon and heard the squeal of the smoke alarm, as it ripped through the room.

Chapter Four

"Dammit!" Mark shut off the flame under the frying pan and turned on a fan that didn't work.

A giggle erupted from Juliet, who sat on the sofa, but he ignored it as he hurried to place the smoking skillet in the sink, dump out the grease and burnt bacon and turn on the faucet. The water hit the hot pan, roaring and sputtering like someone had entered the gates of hell.

As the smoke alarm continued to blast, he looked up at the archaic safety device that didn't have an on or off switch, then swore under his breath as he hurried to open the window, to let fresh air into the room, to allow the smoke to dissipate. All the while, the alarm continued to shriek like a drunken banshee.

By this time, Juliet's giggle turned into a laugh,

triggering a rush of embarrassment. Frustration. And anger at himself for getting distracted.

"What's so funny?" he asked.

Grabbing a dish towel from the countertop, he began fanning the smoke away from the kitchen, hoping it would clear the air and make the stupid alarm shut up. When that didn't seem to work, he reached up, jerked open the plastic contraption and removed the batteries.

Silence.

Except for Juliet's laughter.

When he glanced over his shoulder, he watched her belly jiggle with mirth. "Hey, stop that. Do you want to shake the baby loose?"

She placed a hand on her enlarged womb, as though trying to hold back the tear-provoking laughter, but it didn't work. Between her chuckles, she managed to say, "I assumed you knew how to cook."

"I do. But I'm not used to this stove."

Her gaze scanned the kitchen and lingered on the newspaper spread over the gold Formica countertop— no doubt realizing what he'd been doing when the bacon got away from him.

The editorial had caught his eye, dragging him into small-town politics, the debate about the gold rush, and the fortune hunters who'd converged on Thunder Canyon with hopes of striking it rich.

Consequently, Mark had neglected to watch the stove, the flame, the sizzling meat.

"Anything interesting going on in the world?"

"Undoubtedly," he said. "But I was reading the

Thunder Canyon Nugget, which is chock-full of nothing."

"Well, something obviously caught your attention."

"Not really. The paper, like this town, can't compete with the real world." He turned off the kitchen faucet and nodded toward the sink. "I'm afraid that was the last of the bacon. And the pan needs to go in that Dumpster outside."

"Don't throw it away. There's cleanser and steel wool under the sink."

"I'm not going to scrub this thing." He chucked the pan into the trashcan. "I'll buy you a new one as soon as I get the chance."

She swiped at the moisture under one eye, evidence of her amusement. But she couldn't hide her grin. "I've got cornflakes in the cupboard. And there's a banana on the counter. You can slice it—if you like fruit on your breakfast cereal."

Mark didn't like bananas, didn't like the taste or the texture. He'd eat his cereal plain, although he preferred a manly meal like bacon and eggs.

As he rummaged through the kitchen, looking for bowls and a box of cornflakes, he tried to shake off the image of what would have made a hearty breakfast going up in smoke. Of course, with all the fast food he'd scarfed down in his travels, his body could probably use the fiber from the cereal. Better to flush those arteries than clog them.

"It was really sweet of you to try and cook for me," she said.

Yeah, well, he didn't feel sweet. Or funny. And if

someone downstairs heard that damned alarm and called the fire department, he was going to feel stupid.

A few minutes later, after the smoke had begun to clear, he fixed her cereal, adding the sliced bananas on top. Then he placed her bowl on the coffee table so she wouldn't need to get up and walk any more than necessary.

"Thanks." She tugged at his sleeve, drawing his attention. "And I'm sorry for laughing."

"No you aren't." He tossed her a laid-back grin, sliding back into the easy banter they shared.

"Okay, I'm not." She giggled again. "You should have seen the look on your face when that alarm went off. And the way you frantically swung that dish towel around like a dime-store cowboy trying to lasso the horse that had thrown him."

"I think you enjoyed seeing me screw up."

"Let's say I found it entertaining. I'm competitive by nature. Maybe it's a little sister/big brother thing."

Was she saying she thought of him as a big brother? He supposed that ought to be kind of nice. Or touching. But for some reason it irked him that she thought of him that way. As if he were too old for her to consider as a lover—well, if she weren't having a baby and all.

Nah. She couldn't have been thinking about him as lover material. Mother Nature probably disconnected all the sexual urges when a woman got pregnant. In fact, he doubted Juliet thought about making love at all—especially now.

So why had sex crossed *his* mind—even briefly?

Maybe because it had been a while since he'd had time to spend on a relationship—as noncommittal as his were.

She swung her feet around to the floor and sat up to eat, making room for him to take a seat beside her on the sofa.

Actually, when Mark put his frustration and embarrassment aside, he had to admit it was nice seeing her smile, hearing her laugh. He shot her a crooked grin. "I looked like a cowboy, huh?"

"Roy Rogers at his worst." Her eyes glimmered and her lips twitched, as she used her spoon to snag a slice of banana and pop it in her mouth.

Although he enjoyed a good joke, a part of him didn't like her laughing at him. But he chided himself for being sensitive about something so minor and took a sip of coffee. As he savored the rich brew, he realized he'd done something right this morning.

He glanced at the ceramic cup—white, with a pink carnation trim along the edge. The pattern was bright and cheery, unlike the other things in the house. And he wondered if she'd had a hand in choosing the dishes. "Was the kitchen furnished, too?"

"The dishes are mine. I packed Mrs. Tasker's set in a box and put them in the closet."

Mark looked at his cup. "I'll bet these are nicer than the ones she had."

"I think so. They're not fancy, but they were my grandmother's, so they're special."

Yeah, well he was beginning to think Juliet was

special, too. Over the years, she'd lost her family. Yet she didn't seem beaten.

His gaze dropped to her stomach, to where she carried her child. Why hadn't the father of her baby stepped up to the plate? Why hadn't he wanted a pretty woman like her? Maybe, over time, the guy would change his mind.

"Tell me something," Mark said. "Does the baby's father know where to find you?"

"No." She dabbed her lips with the paper towel he'd given her to use as a napkin.

Mark might not have any desire to be a husband and father, but if Juliet—or rather some other woman—was having his baby, he'd want to know about it. And he'd want to know where she and his child lived. "Don't you think you should tell him? In case he needs to see the baby or send money?"

She thought for a moment, as if trying to find the words to defend her move out of state. Or maybe she was trying to decide whether Mark had been right, whether she ought to let the baby's father know where she was residing.

After studying the pattern on her cereal bowl, she caught his gaze. The bubbly smile that had seemed permanently fixed moments ago had drifted. "I grew up in the barrios of San Diego. But I was raised in a loving home, and we were happy."

He didn't know what that had to do with anything, but he'd been curious about her past. So he shifted in his seat, facing her, letting her know he was interested in what she had to say.

"I never knew my mother. She left home when I was just a baby. But my grandmother moved in to help raise my brother and me."

Mark wasn't sure where she was going with this. Why was she skirting his question?

"My father worked at a neighborhood *tortilleria* to support the family. It was a small, family-owned business that didn't provide health insurance for the employees. And even though my dad insisted Manny and I visit the doctor whenever we were sick, he didn't like spending the money for himself." She paused for a moment, her gaze drifting back to the pink carnation trim on her bowl. "When I was fourteen, he died of cancer. It had been a treatable case that went undetected until it was too late."

"I'm sorry."

"Me, too. But Papa was a man of great faith. And I know he's in Heaven." She offered him a sincere smile, one that held feeling, conviction and victory over grief. "It was tough back then, but Manny and I did all right. We took care of each other. And we held on to the values we'd been taught."

Manny was her older brother, Mark realized. The young man who'd died in an industrial accident. Without meaning to, Mark glanced at the bookshelf, at the silver frame that held a smiling boy in a red baseball uniform.

"About four years ago, after I graduated from high school, I got a job waiting tables in a San Diego suburb at a small Mexican restaurant called La Cocina.

And Manny took a night job as a stock clerk in a discount superstore. We pooled our resources and moved out of the barrio, where we could create a home together and start a new life. We'd dreamed of buying a house. It had been a dream of our father's, then it was ours. Now it's mine."

Juliet, he realized, was made of sturdier stuff than she seemed.

She leaned back into the sofa. "Manny's death was a real blow."

And not just because of his youth, Mark realized. They'd been close. And her brother had been the last family member she had.

Mark struggled not to take her hand, to pull her into his arms. To provide a hug. Something. But he'd never been a touchy-feely kind of guy.

"One of the regulars who frequented the restaurant where I worked, an older guy who was a lawyer, volunteered to help me. To take care of the legalities resulting from my brother's estate and the workman's comp lawsuit that's still pending."

A nice guy? Mark wondered. Or an attorney looking for a cut of a settlement she was bound to get?

Juliet ran a hand over her belly. Over her child. "I needed a friend. Someone to talk to. Someone who cared. And Erik Kramer was a charmer who promised to be there for me. I believed him, and before long, we became lovers." At that point, she looked up, caught Mark's eye. "He was my first."

If the attorney had been in the room, Mark might have considered punching him. Charming a young virgin when she was grieving smacked of unethical behavior. And since she'd already mentioned that the baby's father hadn't wanted the child—or her—it made Kramer seem like more of a jerk.

There was a certain responsibility a man ought to have after taking a woman's virginity, especially when she was vulnerable, as Juliet had been. And the man should have been there for her when the chips were down. Like he'd promised.

"When I found out I was pregnant, I broke the news to him. I knew he'd be surprised. Like I was. But I assumed we'd make the most of it." She offered Mark a wistful smile. "You know. That we'd get married and live happily ever after."

Mark could guess the end of the story. "Apparently, Kramer wasn't into marriage."

"Oh, but he was." Juliet smiled wryly. "He and his wife of fifteen years were planning a Mediterranean cruise to celebrate their wedding anniversary."

Mark might be hell-bent on remaining single after his disappointing divorce, but that didn't mean he approved of married men having affairs. A commitment—if a man or woman were inclined to make one—ought to mean something.

Juliet peered at him with misty eyes. "If Erik would have been honest with me, if I'd known he had a wife, I never would have slept with him. He gave me every reason to believe that he was free to pursue a relationship. That he loved me."

"He lied to you. The guy's a bastard, Juliet." Mark wished Kramer was standing before him so he could knock his lights out. "I hope he's agreed to pay you child support."

"He gave me nearly a thousand dollars in cash, telling me to get rid of the 'problem.' Then he encouraged me to get a little something for myself with what was left over."

Mark reached out, took her hand and gave it a squeeze. But it didn't seem to be enough.

"The pregnancy had come as a surprise to me, too," Juliet said, caressing her womb again. "But there was no way I'd consider aborting my baby. He or she is the only family I have left."

"So you left San Diego. But what about the lawsuit?"

"For that reason, I'll eventually call and give his law firm my address. But I wanted to put some distance between us. Emotionally, as well as physically."

It made sense, he supposed.

"I didn't want the baby to find out that its father didn't want him or her, that he had another family that didn't include us. So I pocketed the money he'd given me, gave notice at La Cocina, had a garage sale, packed my belongings into Manny's truck and headed north. I wasn't sure where I was going, but I was eager to create a family of my own."

"And you ended up in Thunder Canyon."

"I wanted to find a small town where people knew their neighbors, where there were no secrets, no one who could betray my trust."

Mark wasn't so sure she'd found that here, but he wasn't about to splash a wave of cynicism on a young woman struggling to embrace a buoy of hope.

"That's probably way more than you wanted to know," she said. "But I didn't want you to think I'd intentionally hook up with a married man. That I'd normally be that stupid. That my father and the church hadn't taught me better than that."

Mark flicked a strand of hair away from her cheek, and cupped her jaw. His thumb made a slow, gentle stroke of her skin. "You're a special lady, Juliet. And someday, a lucky man is going to figure that out. And then you'll have a family again, the family you deserve."

Funny thing was, Mark the cynic actually believed that to be true.

For her.

But unlike pretty Juliet, a family wasn't in his cards. He'd tried to recreate his broken family once, but his ex had doused that dream years ago.

Not about to go another round with the kitchen or the stove for at least another day, Mark ordered two take-out dinners from The Hitching Post. He hoped Juliet would be pleased with his choice—pork chops, mashed potatoes and gravy, green beans and lemon meringue pie.

He carried the cartons of food upstairs and, while Juliet turned off the television, set the dinette table. The doctor had said she could get up to use the bathroom, so Mark figured it wouldn't hurt to sit for a couple of minutes.

As he poured them two glasses of milk, she crossed her arms over her belly and arched a brow. "What? No bourbon?"

"Not tonight."

It's not as though Mark was a lush, even though he could understand why she might think so. She'd seen him having nightly cocktails ever since he'd arrived in town. But that was liquid courage to face the memories he couldn't seem to shake while in Thunder Canyon.

And this evening, he had an intriguing young woman to keep his thoughts off his past. Off the rebellion that had led to his sister's death.

Juliet reached for a butter horn roll, tore off a piece and popped it in her mouth. When she swallowed, she placed her elbows on the table and leaned forward. "So, tell me about the assignment that's going to write itself."

"Actually, it's going to be a big spread. A Sunday paper special."

"Impressive." She smiled, and he felt a surge of pride, of pleasure. "What kind of spread? What will be the focus?"

"I'm going to write about the gold rushes, past and present. The willingness of naive miners to pursue a hopeless dream."

"Why not focus on the positive, on the excitement, the thrill of striking it rich?"

Maybe because Mark's hopes and dreams had died in Thunder Canyon, and he'd had to move away to get his life back. To make a future for himself.

"Do you realize how many miners actually hit pay dirt?" he asked.

"Some do. That's what makes it so exciting, so interesting."

"Come on, Juliet. You really don't believe anyone

is going to find any significant amount of gold in Thunder Canyon, do you? By the early 1900s, the mines in the area had played out."

She took a bite of the crab apple garnish. "There could be another vein of gold. And someone might find it."

"Do those rose-colored glasses ever fog up?"

A grin tugged at her lips, creating a dimple on one cheek. "I choose to look on the bright side of life."

That was growing more and more apparent. "The chance of a big strike is pretty slim. Ever since the 1860s, when the first gold rush started in this area, miners swept the hills, finding nuggets here and there. And yes, some people did get rich. But there weren't too many big fortunes made for the little guys. And most people were disappointed, if not devastated after gambling their savings on lady luck."

"You're more pessimistic than most of the people around here."

She wasn't the first woman to point out his cynicism. But he liked to think of himself as realistic.

"When I was in high school, I wrote a paper on Fourteen Mile City, a stretch of settlements amidst the gold fields." Mark had received an A+ on that report, along with a budding interest in journalism. "My history teacher praised me for pointing out the downside of mining and exposing what greed did to people. Back then, gullible investors bought stock in fraudulent ventures, sometimes bankrupting themselves. And I won't even go into what the gold rush cost the Indians and the Chinese."

"I can see that there's a downside. But I think most people would rather read about dreams, possibilities, hopes."

"The best I can do is write realistically. But it should make you feel better to know that I'm going to also include the history and the legends of Thunder Canyon." He stole a glance at her.

A growing fascination lit her face. "What kind of legends?"

"Supposedly, this canyon was sacred to the Indians, although I'll have to research that for accuracy. And there's also that story about Amos Douglas winning the Queen of Hearts gold mine in a poker game."

Juliet turned toward him, brushing her knees against his thigh, shooting a tingle of warmth and awareness through his blood. The way she looked at him, her eyes wide, hanging on his every word, made him puff up like a toad that thought he was king of the pond.

"Was Amos related to Jason and Caleb Douglas?" she asked.

"Yeah. Amos was the original Douglas settler in Thunder Canyon."

"And what's the story about the poker game? Who did Amos win it from?"

"I don't know. Maybe a prospector with a drinking and gambling problem. It's hard to say. When I get some time, I'm going to head over to the museum and see if they've got more information."

She sobered. "I'm sorry, Mark."

"About what?"

"Keeping you from your research."

"Don't worry about it. I can place a few calls, if necessary, and can research the Internet. Maybe by the time I get back to my interviews, Caleb will have found the deed." His explanation seemed to appease her, and he was glad, although not entirely sure why.

She placed a finger to her lips and clamped down on a nail, puzzled by something. "If the Douglas family owned the gold mine property, what do you think happened to the deed?"

Mark shrugged. "Who knows? It's been over a hundred years. Maybe Amos or one of his descendents misplaced it. They probably thought the land wasn't worth anything."

"Not even in sentimental value?"

He reached up, stroked a silky strand of her raven-black hair and gave it a gentle tug. "Most people see land for what it is. Real estate. Money in the pocket."

"I'm not most people."

"So I'm learning." For a moment, something passed between them. Something tender and intimate. Something that ought to scare the hell out of him. Something that *did*. He dropped his hand and studied his empty plate.

"Well," she began, "from what I've gathered from mealtime chitchat at The Hitching Post, Caleb seems more focused on finding that deed than in the ground-breaking of the ski resort he's developing."

"He's probably no different than the others. Each time another gold nugget is found, folks want to believe there's an untapped vein out there. The idea of sudden riches stirs the blood of some people."

"But not yours?"

"No."

"What stirs your blood?"

He looked at her, caught the gold flecks in her eyes that glimmered in the lamplight when she teased him, spotted the cute nose that turned up slightly. Noticed the fullness of her bottom lip, the softness that begged to be kissed.

His blood was moving along at a pretty good clip now, but he'd be damned if he'd let her know that.

Damn. He definitely needed to get laid. How long had it been? Surely not long enough for his libido to contemplate putting the moves on an expectant mother, for cripes sake.

"You really are a stick in the mud." She patted his thigh in a gentle, we're-good-friends way. But it didn't seem to matter to the rush of his bloodstream. "You have no imagination, Mark. Can't you tap into your heart?"

His heart had fizzled out a long time ago. After his sister had died. And whatever had been left shriveled up when his wife filed for divorce and moved out of their apartment while he was away on an assignment.

Juliet tugged on the sleeve of his shirt again, which seemed to be her habit. Her way of touching him without actually doing so.

"Can't you let go once in a while?" she asked.

Let what go?

His past? His guilt? His pessimism?

"What do you mean? I know how to have fun." At least, he used to. It had been a while—about as long as it had been since he'd had a wild passionate, no-strings-attached night.

"Close your eyes," she said.

"Why?"

"Just do it."

For some dumb reason, he did. "Okay, now what?"

"Think about The Hitching Post. About a building that's been around for ages. Can't you almost hear the plunking sound of a piano? The voices of people who once lived and played here?"

He squinted, opening one eye and then the other. "I'm not sure we ought to be listening to *those* voices. This floor was a brothel, remember?" He chuckled. "Did you still want me to imagine the tales these walls could tell?"

Her face flushed, although the Pollyanna glimmer remained in those mahogany eyes. And she shrugged. "It might be interesting."

"Interesting?"

"I thought most women in the olden days didn't particularly like sex."

"I'm sure plenty of them did." He grinned. "What makes you think they didn't?"

"Well, once when I was in the fourth grade, I overheard my *abuelita* and an older neighbor lady talking about sex."

"Oh, yeah?"

"My grandmother said she wouldn't walk across the room for it."

"That's too bad. It sounds as though your grandfather didn't know how to pleasure her."

Juliet didn't respond. But then, what was there to say?

Mark wondered whether Kramer had been good to her, whether he'd given her the kind of first-time experience she should have had. "Tell me, Juliet. Would *you* walk across the room for it?"

"Probably. If there wasn't anything good on television." Her eyes glimmered, and he couldn't tell if she was serious or pulling his leg.

"Then Kramer wasn't any better at pleasing a lady than your grandfather was," Mark said, taking a guess.

Her eyes widened, as if he'd hit the G-spot and set off her first orgasm.

Sexual awareness filled the room, settling over him. Over her, too, he suspected.

Her lips parted in an enticing way, almost as if inviting him to close in on her, to give her the kind of kiss that made blood pound, race, demand.

What was happening to him?

He ought to pull away. Let it go. Laugh it off, like a guy with any sense would.

But Mark had never been very heroic.

And when Juliet ran the tip of her tongue along her lips, he was lost.

Chapter Five

The kiss started innocently, sweetly. A tender promise of sugar and spice.

But before Mark could decide whether to pull back or press on, Juliet placed an angel-soft hand on his cheek and leaned forward—into the kiss.

Her lips, parted, and he savored the taste of her, a unique, tantalizing flavor that went beyond a hint of lemon and meringue. He cupped her jaw with one hand, fingers delving toward the back of her neck, the strands of her hair brushing his knuckles in a silky cascade.

As the kiss intensified, ever so slowly, his tongue explored the wet velvety softness of her mouth, tentatively seeking and savoring until he craved more of whatever captivated his senses.

Desire smoldered under the surface, warming his blood in a steady rush, urging him to give it free rein, to let it build and surge.

But something ensnared him, held him in a mesmerizing spell that slowed their motions, while intensifying sensual awareness.

Whatever it was seemed to have caught her, too, he realized, as she whimpered softly and her fingers threaded through his hair.

So much for Mother Nature disconnecting sexual urges in women who were in her condition.

Oh, for cripes sake.

Her condition.

She was *pregnant.* And he was supposed to be taking care of her, making sure she took it easy—not doing something reckless that could jeopardize her health.

He broke the kiss, his hand dropping to his side, useless and empty. "I'm sorry, Juliet. That was crazy. Stupid. And so damn out of line."

"That's okay. I lost my head, too."

That was obvious, as well as unexpected—just as his impulsive response had been. He wasn't sure what had come over them, but his libido had been primed and ready to rock.

A mischievous sparkle lit her eyes, as a slow smile curled her lips. "And just for the record, that kiss was definitely something I'd walk across the room for."

He didn't know if he should feel flattered or guiltridden. In self-defense, he thought about changing the subject, but his male pride wouldn't let him ignore what she'd said. "So you liked my kiss, huh?"

The twinkle in her eyes intensified, highlighting the flush of her cheeks. "Yes, I did like it."

A goofy urge to pound on his chest Tarzan style swept over him. He tried to laugh it off with what sounded to him like a dorky chuckle. "That's probably because the television is off and there aren't any TV specials to distract you."

"Maybe," she said, her eyes glazed with…

With what?

Passion? Embarrassment? Annoyance at him for making light of the inappropriate but sensual kiss they'd just shared?

He wasn't sure. But if things were different, if she were someone else, someone not so young—so virginal in spite of her condition—he would have kissed her again, just to see where it led.

But things *weren't* different.

She was expecting a child. And nesting in Thunder Canyon, while Mark couldn't pack his bags and leave town fast enough. Getting involved with Juliet, romantically speaking, was senseless.

So what kind of fool would be tempted to put the moves on her, even if it was one little kiss?

A jerk of a fool who wasn't much better than that married attorney who'd jumped her bones when she was just as vulnerable as she was now.

He raked a hand through his hair. "Listen, I've got to go back to the Wander-On Inn."

"Why? I thought you were spending the night here."

Was she disappointed that he might leave?

Or pleased?

And why, pray tell, should he care either way?

Hell, he really ought to sleep at the inn. Things were way too awkward here. Kissing Juliet had triggered a flight-or-fight response.

She nodded toward the bathroom. "It's just that you left your shaving kit in there."

Yeah. He had. Packed, zipped and ready for a fast getaway. He caught her gaze, saw the question in her eyes. The vulnerability.

Oh, God. What if she went into labor? There wouldn't be anyone with her. And Mark couldn't take that risk.

"I'll be right back," he told her. "I just need to get my laptop so I can do some research on the Internet this evening."

What a crock that was, but her nod told him she'd bought his explanation.

"Take your time," she said. "I'll just leave the door open."

"I don't plan to be gone that long." He just needed a breath of fresh air, a little break. Something he could focus on, other than a casual kiss that didn't mean anything.

"All right. If I'm not on the sofa, I'll be reading in my room."

"I'll just let myself in." He stood and shoved his hands in his pockets, then forced a smile before heading downstairs.

But the "meaningless" kiss followed him, taunting him long after he shut the door and sucked in a deep breath of crisp night air.

* * *

Several minutes after Mark left, Juliet continued to stare at the closed door, her fingers pressed softly to her lips.

What had just happened?

She wasn't sure, but it was more than the kiss that had her heart and mind singing. It was her response to it. That and the overwhelming urge to kiss Mark again. To make sure she hadn't imagined how sweet, how special, how arousing his mouth had been.

Mark's kiss had been so different from those Erik had given her.

Erik's mouth and tongue had been urgent, insistent. The kind of kisses that took her a while to warm up to. On the other hand, Mark, who seemed to know exactly what he was doing, had taken things slow and easy.

She hadn't been lying when she'd told Mark that she'd *probably* walk across the room for sex. It had been nice with Erik. Pleasant, once she caught up to his speed. But more than the act itself, she'd enjoyed the intimacy. The embrace, the touch of someone she'd cared about. But now Erik's lovemaking skills paled.

If the promise in Mark's kiss was an indication of what had been lacking in Erik's, Juliet suspected making love with Mark might prove to be very special indeed. A stimulating opportunity she'd not only walk across the room for, but, in anticipation, would turn off a perfectly good television show along the way.

But how likely was that?

Her hand slowly dropped to her swollen womb, reminding her to focus on motherhood and the new baby she'd soon hold in her arms.

But if Juliet weren't pregnant, she might be tempted to find out what Mark knew about pleasuring a lady that Erik hadn't known.

The next morning, Juliet woke to the aroma of fresh-brewed coffee.

Mark was proving to be an intriguing man, in spite of his cynical nature. The kind of man who made a woman smile when he wasn't around. The kind of man who provoked dreams of romance.

But Juliet knew better than to let silly romantic notions do anything but drift by the wayside. She and Mark had nothing in common.

So why had she spent so much time thinking about him last night? Dreaming about long, lingering kisses that stirred the blood and made her want to slip on a pair of track shoes so she could sprint across the room for another taste of his lips?

She blew out a sigh and climbed from bed. What was wrong with her? She didn't have any business thinking about Mark, his kiss or romance.

For goodness' sake, she was going to be a mother. And if she ever became involved with any one else, it would be with a man who'd make a good husband and father. A man who would take pride in his wife and child while barbecuing in the backyard on Sundays. Someone who held the same family values that she did.

And Mark Anderson, a pessimist who disliked Thunder Canyon and wasn't concerned over the falling out he'd had with his parents, wouldn't fit the bill.

Sure, he'd been good to her, a true friend. He'd also been a great listener, although he hadn't told her very much about himself.

Maybe she ought to quiz him a bit. Find out about the rift he'd had with his parents. Then maybe she could help facilitate a reconciliation.

Families were special.

More than anyone, Juliet knew that. And, if she could get Mark to see the value of a nurturing, loving support system, it would be one way to pay him back for being so good to her.

She slipped on her blue robe and strode into the living area, where he sat at the dinette table, his laptop open, a coffee cup at his side.

"Hey," he said, offering her a smile. "Sleep okay?"

Not really. She'd stewed for way too long about the kiss they'd shared—so long that she couldn't get into that book on pregnancy and childbirth she'd picked up at the library last Saturday. But there was no way she'd make a confession like that. "I slept all right. How about you?"

He glanced at the sofa, where the folded blanket rested on his pillow. "Not bad."

She noticed that he'd taken a shower and shaved. His hair, a bit long and unruly, was still damp. He'd put on a fresh white T-shirt and a pair of worn jeans, but his feet were bare.

He'd made himself at home, which was interesting. Comforting, she supposed.

In the six months she'd dated Erik, he'd never spent the night. Never made a pot of coffee. Never left a shaving kit in her bathroom. She hadn't thought anything about it at the time. Nor had she realized he'd been holding back on their relationship.

So, in a way, it pleased her to know that Mark had settled in, that he'd slept on the sofa. That he'd felt comfortable enough to take a shower in her bathroom. That he'd carefully put away his things, zipping the small leather bag closed. How neat and thoughtful was that?

With the morning sun at his back, blessing him in a glowing aura, he looked as though he belonged here—in her living room with his work spread out in front of him.

He scooted his chair back, the metal legs snagging on the matted green carpet. "I can fix cereal again. And after you've eaten, I'll head to the market and do some shopping."

"Okay." She made her way into the room, taking a seat at the table, and nodded at his laptop computer. "How's the research going?"

"I guess it's going all right. I'm learning some things about the early days of Thunder Canyon, things I remember my history teacher telling us in school. Things I didn't care about back then."

"What kind of things *did* you care about?" she asked, wanting to know more about Mark, his youth, his life.

"Football. Parties. Girls." He slid her a wry smile.

"The stuff that an adolescent surge of testosterone produces."

She returned his smile, as if she understood the typical teenage lifestyle. But she hadn't gotten caught up in any high school activities. Not when she was working after class let out so she could help Manny pay the bills.

"Were you a good student?" she asked.

"Not as good as my dad thought I should be."

Ah, an opening she could zero in on. "I'm sure he was proud of you, too."

"Not that I can remember." The sixties-style dinette chair squeaked, as Mark leaned back in his seat and stretched out his feet. "My mom said that from the time I chucked my first bottle out of the playpen, my dad and I were constantly butting heads."

"What kind of things did you argue about?"

"Everything. About my grades. The way I swung the bat during a Little League game. The hairstyle I chose. The music I listened to. The friends I had. My lazy-ass attitude around the house."

Was the relationship between Mark and his dad just a normal part of adolescent rebellion? A result of that surge of testosterone he'd mentioned earlier?

If that were the case, would their relationship be better now—if given a chance to start fresh?

She placed her elbows on the table and leaned forward, as far as her belly would allow. "Now that you're grown, do you think that maybe your father had a point about any of those things?"

He paused for a while, pondering her question, she supposed. Or maybe reevaluating his memories.

"He was right about my attitude. But it was tough to live with constant criticism, and eventually I got sick and tired of it."

"So you rebelled."

"That's about the size of it. But things got worse after he uprooted the family. My sister and I wanted to stay in Texas with my grandmother."

"Why did he decide to move here?"

"Because some great-uncle we'd never met died and left my dad a motel at the edge of town and a cabin-style home about ten miles up Turner Grade." Mark shook his head. "And to make matters worse, my dad insisted upon living in the mountains. It was hard not having neighbors, especially when my parents were in town all the time."

"I can see how it would have been more convenient for everyone involved if they'd lived closer to the motel."

"Yeah, well that was just another thing we argued about. And even though I think my mother agreed with me, she didn't press him about it."

"And so you're holding all that over his head now?"

Mark tensed. "That and a few other things."

"Like what?"

He fiddled with the keyboard of his computer, as though he hadn't heard her. And she wondered if the discussion was over on his part.

Then, as if her question wasn't still lingering in the air, he signed off the Internet and shut down the computer. "I'm starving. Are you ready for a bowl of cereal?"

"I guess so."

"Good. Once I fix your breakfast, I'll do the laundry. I'm running out of clothes, and I figure you are, too."

"You're not going to do my laundry," she said without thinking. If Mark didn't help her with it, who would? She was supposed to stay off her feet, and she didn't think the doctor would approve of even a simple activity like throwing her clothes into a washer and dryer.

"What are you going to do?" he asked. "Wait until your clothes are all dirty and buy new ones?"

She couldn't do that. But she felt funny about him washing her things, especially her bras and panties. Maybe she could set her undies aside and wash them in the bathroom sink. That wouldn't be any more strenuous than washing her hands, would it?

"Now that we've got that settled," he said, "do you want cornflakes again? Or the granola stuff?"

Apparently, he'd decided not to try and cook again. And she got the feeling he wasn't comfortable in a kitchen. He probably ate all of his meals out. But she was getting tired of cereal every morning.

"A toasted bagel and cream cheese sounds good for a change."

"Okay."

She watched as he puttered around the kitchen, preparing breakfast.

He'd been so good to her. Just like Manny or her father would have been.

When the baby was here and life was back to normal, she'd cook for him. That is, if he was still in Thunder Canyon.

Maybe she shouldn't hold back her thanks. "I appreciate what you've done for me, Mark."

"No problem." He pulled the jug of milk from the fridge. "You don't have anyone else to look after you."

And neither did he, which was sad, especially since his parents were still alive and nearby.

She realized he was avoiding them, something that didn't feel right to her. She opened her mouth to quiz him again, but thought better of it. For now anyway.

In a day or so, she'd bring it up again, because she intended to learn more about that falling-out they'd had. And given the chance, she would encourage him to mend that rift.

Mark might balk at her interference, but she was only looking out for his own good.

Juliet and Manny might have loved each other and been close, but they hadn't always seen eye to eye. But it was love that held a family together, in spite of the differences of opinion.

If anyone knew how to handle stubborn men when they were wrong, Juliet did. And she knew how to get her point across.

Especially when it was in a man's best interests.

For the next couple of days, Juliet let the subject of Mark's family ride. But on Saturday afternoon, after he'd gone across the street to the inn to check for telephone messages, she realized she couldn't avoid it any longer.

When he entered the apartment, he wore a blue flannel shirt under a brown leather jacket, which he peeled off and hung on the coat tree by the door. "I never could get used to this unpredictable Montana weather. It's supposed to be spring. But I swear we're in for another storm."

"Did you get what you needed at the inn?"

"Yeah." He kicked off his shoes, then checked the thermostat.

"You know," she began. "Something is puzzling me."

"What's that?"

"You told me that after that falling-out you'd made peace with your family."

"We talk." He strode toward the window and peered outside.

"Then why, if your folks own the Big Sky Motel, are you patronizing the Wander-On Inn?"

He turned and crossed his arms. "Because the inn is more convenient. It's in the middle of town."

That might be true. But she knew there was more to it than that. "Have you seen your parents yet?"

His movements slowed; his expression tensed. "No. I haven't had time."

But why had he been able to find time to come into The Hitching Post each evening and chill out at the bar first?

"Have you called them?" she asked.

He shrugged and headed for the kitchen. "I talked to my mother a week or so ago."

"Maybe you ought to drop by the motel for a visit."

"They're pretty busy." He opened the refrigerator and pulled out a can of soda.

"Do you know what I think? That the falling-out isn't over at all."

"So what if it's not?" He pulled the tab and took a long, steady swig before setting the can on the countertop. "Not every family is close, Juliet. And some of us prefer it that way."

"How about your sister? Do you talk to her?"

He stiffened, then touched the hole on the top on the aluminum can, his index finger circling the sharp edge. "My sister is dead."

"I'm sorry. How did it happen?"

He caught her gaze, but didn't speak. His eyes swept down to her lap, where her hands rested around the bulge of her tummy.

He finally said, "It doesn't matter."

"Why not?"

The muscles in his cheek twitched, and his jaw tensed, as though he was holding back.

"Were the two of you close?"

He shrugged again, but the tension didn't leave his face. "I guess so."

Juliet had told him about Manny's death. Her dad's, too. So it seemed only fair to ask. "Was it an accident?"

The question hung in the air, making it hard for Mark to breathe. "Yeah. It was an accident."

And it had been. Sort of. Mark hadn't meant to screw up. But he wasn't going to go there, wasn't going to discuss it with Juliet.

"That's too bad," she said.

Yeah. It was.

She probably figured it was a car accident or something like that. But Mark wouldn't correct her. Hell, even if he felt like opening up, revealing his guilt and pain, an expectant mother sure as hell didn't need to hear how his sister and her unborn baby died during labor.

"If you're the only child your parents have left, I imagine they would welcome a reconciliation."

How could she be so damn optimistic all the time? So naive?

"Things are more complicated than that," he explained. "More complex. And I'd rather not talk about it."

"Families are a blessing, Mark."

Oh, for cripes sake. Why couldn't she just let it go? Quit nagging at him?

He didn't need a ration of guilt to upset his lunch. To ruin a quiet afternoon.

"Why don't you approach them first? Maybe ask them out to dinner?"

Mark bristled. He'd kept his guilty secret bottled up inside for so long that he wasn't going to relive it, not even in dialogue.

"You know what?" he asked her. "I've got cabin fever. Maybe I ought to take a walk before it starts snowing." As he made his way to the door, she followed, grabbing him by the sleeve of his flannel shirt.

"I'm sorry, Mark. I'm just trying to help."

"Well, don't." He raked a hand through his hair. "I need some fresh air."

As he reached the doorknob, she sucked in a breath. His feet slowed, but he kept a forward motion.

"Oh, my God," she said. "Wait."

He turned to acknowledge her voice—not her command—but she was looking down, her lips parted, her eyes fixed on a dribble of water running down her legs.

A gush splattered on the floor, and she looked up at him, eyes wide and frightened. "My water broke."

Chapter Six

Mark wasn't exactly sure what "my water broke" meant, especially when a woman had a good month or so to go. But it couldn't be good.

A jolt of fear shot through him, reminding him of his sister's death, of how he'd failed her. Reminding him of his recklessness. His guilt. "I'll call 9-1-1."

"Doc Emerson told me to call his office if something like this happened."

"Isn't he the guy who had the heart attack?"

She nodded, her eyes transfixed on the floor, on the wet puddle.

"If your doctor is still in ICU, he's not going to be any help. Isn't there someone on call for him?"

"Yes," she said. "But I don't know him very well. Maybe if I go to Thunder Canyon General, Doctor

Hart will be working. I'd feel better if she were in charge."

"I don't care who we see, as long as he or she has a medical degree. Come on." He grabbed her jacket from the coat tree and held it open as she slipped her arms inside. He wanted to bundle her up, even though it wasn't that cold outside, but there was no way he would be able to button it around her stomach.

As he reached for the doorknob, she asked him to wait. "I'd better get some towels to sit on. And the overnight bag. It's already packed and in the closet."

"I'll get them." He wasn't going to waste any time getting her to the hospital. Wasn't going to risk something going wrong before he placed her under a doctor's care.

When Mark had the towels and the gray canvas bag, he opened the door, then paused on the stoop. "Should I carry you down?"

"No. That's okay. The stairs aren't going to be too strenuous for me. The baby is coming now. Let me walk."

He wasn't sure what to do, but at this point, she sounded kind of confident. And since he was scared spitless, he thought it best to defer to her—as long as they were hospital-bound.

Mark followed her down the creaking stairs, his feet hitting the steps like he had on a pair of ski boots. The afternoon sun had broken through the clouds, melting whatever snow had been left the night before. Maybe spring was really on its way. He was ready for green buds, warmer days and the kind of sunshine that made a guy want to be out-doors.

As she reached the white sedan, he opened the pas-senger door and waited for her to adjust the towels. So far, so good.

"Are you sure the baby's coming?" he asked.

"Yes. Once the water breaks, contractions are more or less imminent. And according to the pregnancy book I've been reading, they won't try to stop labor this time."

A million fears hit him in the gut, nearly knocking him breathless, and all he could think of was getting her to the hospital, of passing the baton to medical professionals. Yet at the same time, he wanted to pro-tect her, keep her safe—not an easy task for a man who meant to remain detached.

He circled the car to get in on the driver's side, his heart pounding in his ears, stirring his fear, as well as his reluctance to be involved. He stole a glance at her, saw her pursed lips, her furrowed brow. She had to be more frightened than he was.

As they pulled out onto Main, her breath caught and she rubbed her stomach.

"What's the matter?" he asked, hoping she hadn't heard the panicky edge to his voice.

"I'm having a contraction."

Oh, no. He'd read horror stories of kids being born in taxis and cars. But surely they didn't just pop out. Didn't the labor process take a while?

He glanced at his wristwatch, then stepped on the gas, trying his best to zip through the lazy Saturday afternoon traffic. A lady honked at him, and he had half a notion to flip her off, shake a fist and swear at her. But he had to admit he hadn't seen her vehicle, hadn't realized he'd cut her off.

Damn. He'd better slow down and get his head out of his ass. A car accident wouldn't do Juliet or the baby any good. But he didn't want to waste precious time and found it hard not to speed.

As they turned onto White Water Drive, his pulse seemed to settle into a steady rush, rather than a frantic race. He stole a look at her, saw the apprehension in her eyes.

Do something, he told himself. *Make her feel better.*

Hell, he had to do something to make them *both* feel better. But he didn't have a clue what.

He gripped the steering wheel as though he could control the situation as well as he maneuvered the rented sedan.

Up ahead, he spotted the colorful flags that lined the entrance of Ranch View Estates, the development that she'd pointed out to him the last time they'd traveled this road.

"How big are those homes?" he asked, hoping to stir up a conversation that might take her mind off her worries. Off his, too.

She looked out the window, but her face didn't light up. Not like it had when she'd first made a fuss over the housing development and mentioned that she'd gone to see the models. "I'm not sure. I think the smallest one is about twenty-eight hundred square feet."

"How many bedrooms?" he asked, trying his damnedest to keep the casual conversation going.

"Three to four, I think. The biggest model has a den that can be used as an office or another bedroom."

"Those sure are nice-size lots. I guess a guy would have to buy a good mower."

She nodded, her eyes fixed on something he couldn't see.

But Mark continued to keep up the lame conversation. "And I like the ranch-style architecture."

"Uh-huh."

"It sure would be nice living in a gated community." That is, if he ever got the urge to put down roots. Then it would be nice.

She started rubbing her belly with her hand and breathing weird. Was that normal?

He glanced at his watch again. They'd been on the road for about five minutes. Only three or four more miles to go. Then he could pass the responsibility on to someone else. He tried to think up something else to say, but what was the use? He had a feeling she didn't appreciate his efforts to chat, and they were almost at the hospital.

Moments later, they pulled into the entrance of Thunder Canyon General. By this time, Mark knew the drill, but that didn't make him feel any less nervous. Any less afraid.

As he parked the idling car under the covered portico, Juliet reached a hand across the seat and tugged at the sleeve of his leather jacket. "Thanks for bringing me here."

"No problem."

Had voicing her appreciation been her way of letting him off the hook? Of telling him he could just leave her here?

He hoped so. But he'd wait until he got her settled, until the doctor stepped in and took over. Then he could walk out the door and get on with his life, knowing he'd done his good deed. That he'd made sure at least one pregnant woman had gotten to the hospital safely.

Moments later, Mark brought a nurse and a wheelchair to the car. And for the first time in what felt like forever, he was able to hand over Juliet to someone medically trained. Someone competent.

Still, he followed her and the nurse through the double glass doors, past the security guard. Mark acknowledged the uniformed man, and the guy nodded in return.

While the E.R. clerk handled the paperwork and phoned the maternity ward to give them a heads-up, Mark continued to hang out, to make sure the admission process was complete and that Juliet didn't need him anymore.

"Who's the head of the department?" Mark asked, wanting the best for Juliet.

"Dr. Chester is the head of Ob-Gyn," the clerk responded. "She's out of town on a speaking engagement at the Montana Women's Health Fair. But Dr. Hart is here."

"Oh, good," Juliet said. "I was hoping Dr. Hart would be working."

As long as she was comfortable with the resident, Mark supposed it was okay. But he'd have felt better with the head obstetrician.

Before long, a heavyset man dressed in hospital greens stepped behind Juliet's wheelchair to take her to the elevator and up to the second floor.

She glanced at Mark. "Are you going with us?"

It was just a question, he told himself. Not a request. He could tell her he'd take a rain check this time around. Besides, it was a perfect time to cut whatever flimsy connection they'd built over the past few days, a perfect chance to escape before she expected something from him. Something he couldn't— or wouldn't—provide.

But what if she wasn't out of the woods yet? What if she needed him—or rather someone—to be with her for a little while?

"Yeah," he told her. "I'll stay for a bit."

She nodded, as the orderly pushed her down the hall, and Mark fell into step behind them.

When they reached the heavy double doors that required someone to buzz them in, the orderly pulled the wheelchair to a stop.

"What's the deal with the password and the locked door?" Mark asked.

"A year or so ago, a woman tried to kidnap one of the newborns. She didn't get away with it, but we tightened our security, hoping to prevent something like that from ever happening again." The orderly punched in a code, and the doors swung open.

Mark glanced at Juliet and saw the wide-eyed

expression. Was she concerned that someone might try to take her little one?

"You and the baby will be just fine," Mark told her.

Then he forced a smile, hoping to high heaven that what he'd told her was true.

When Dr. Hart donned a pair of gloves, Mark slipped out of the birthing room. Juliet wondered whether he'd say goodbye before leaving. There wasn't any reason for him to stay, she supposed.

She held her breath, waiting as Dr. Hart examined her.

"You're about two to three centimeters dilated already," the doctor said. "And the head has dropped down nicely."

"But it's too soon for me to deliver." Nervous fear shot through her. "Is the baby going to be all right?"

"I think everything is going to be fine, even though it's more than four weeks early. When you were here last Sunday, we gave you medication to help the lungs develop. And we've managed to keep the baby in the womb for nearly a week. At this stage, every day helps." The doctor placed a hand on Juliet's shoulder. "Don't worry, Mom. We'll do our best to get that baby delivered safely and in your arms."

Juliet wasn't sure if Mark had already left the hospital or if he was waiting outside the room until after she'd been examined. Of course, she couldn't blame him for leaving—if he had. And it was okay. She'd never planned on having a birth coach or anyone to support her during labor.

But when Dr. Hart stepped out of the room and Mark popped his head inside the door, she felt a rush of relief.

He made his way to her bedside. "How's it going?"

"I'm nervous," she admitted. "And scared."

"Are you hurting?"

"It's tolerable."

He took the seat beside the bed. When the back of his chair swayed in movement, a little-boy smile lit his face. "Hey, it rocks."

Before she could respond, Beth Ann, the dark-haired nurse she'd had last time, entered the room. She greeted them, then started an IV and hooked up a monitor to Juliet's tummy.

Mark looked a bit sheepish at first, but before long he was asking questions about the screen that graphed the baby's heart rate and another squiggly line that reflected the length and duration of the contractions.

"What's normal for the baby's heart rate?" he asked Beth Ann.

"She's sleeping, so one-twenty seems to be normal for her. But when she wakes up, that will increase to one-forty or so. And you'll see some little black lines along this area that will indicate her movements." The nurse handed Juliet a remote call button. "I'll leave you two alone for a while. And I'll come back and check on you in about two hours."

"You're leaving for two hours?" Mark stood and raked a hand through his hair. "What if something goes wrong?"

Beth Ann smiled. "We're constantly monitoring

her from the nurse's station. We can see this screen in there. And if anything changes, I'll be right in."

Mark shoved his hands in his pockets. A grimace indicated he wasn't pleased that the nurse was leaving. He slid a look at the monitor.

"Hey, wait," he called to Beth Ann. "There was a little green light that looked like a bell. And now it's yellow. What does that mean?"

"It means that something is happening in one of the other birthing rooms."

"Is someone in trouble now?" he asked.

"It doesn't necessarily mean trouble. It means that something is happening. In this case, the woman in birthing room three is being prepped for delivery."

"Oh." His words indicated understanding, but his expression was clearly one of concern, worry. He glanced at Juliet, a fish-out-of-water expression in his eyes.

She would have loved to have taken a picture of him at that moment, something to keep forever. But another dull pain began in her back, then spread to her stomach, as the womb that had once sheltered her baby began to force the child out into the world.

Juliet closed her eyes, breathing with the contraction like she'd learned from the birthing video she'd checked out of the library. She wasn't sure whether the Lamaze techniques worked or not, but it did keep her mind focused on something other than the pain.

"It's winding down," Mark said, coaching her to hang on, to stay on top.

He'd said he would stay for "a bit," and she appreciated whatever time he shared with her.

But that didn't mean she wouldn't miss him when he decided to leave.

Thirty minutes later, Mark had gotten into the swing of the labor routine. He kept track of the contractions, telling Juliet when to expect another, when a pain was peaking and when it was starting to ease. He even found himself breathing with her, which was probably goofy. But what the heck?

More than once, he thought of his sister, Kelly. Thought of her going through this by herself. Alone. Frightened. In pain. Bleeding.

But if he focused on that, if he allowed the guilt to slip back in, he'd drive himself crazy. So he forced the image from his mind, zeroing in on the petite woman who held his hand and the child who was struggling to be born.

Time was measured by the minute lines on the monitor, as Juliet's contractions came quicker and lasted longer. Still, he repeatedly looked at the clock, hoping the two hours would be up and the nurse would return. Juliet was really hurting, and he hoped they would give her something to ease her pain.

As the door creaked open, Beth Ann entered the room. "I think I'd better check you. Your contractions are getting closer and appear to be quite strong."

"I hope I'm four centimeters," Juliet said. "Dr. Hart said she'd order an epidural then."

Mark stood, but instead of leaving, he pulled the

curtain, giving Juliet privacy. Surprisingly, he was feeling more comfortable about being in the room. And she seemed to be glad he was there and had thanked him more than once.

About an hour ago, she'd asked him to massage the small of her back, something she'd said helped. So they'd fallen into a routine. Each time a contraction started, she'd roll to her side and he'd rub until the pain eased.

"Well, I'll be darned," Beth Ann said.

"What's wrong?" Mark flung back the curtain and stepped forward, just as the nurse was removing her gloves. "That was quick, Juliet. You're almost eight centimeters dilated."

"What's that mean?" Mark asked.

"It means I'm in transition," Juliet said. "And it's too late for an epidural."

"It also means her labor is progressing faster than usual, especially for a first baby. I'd better call Dr. Hart. It could be a quick delivery."

Mark's heart dropped to the floor. The baby was coming?

Now?

The nurse hadn't seemed too worried, but then she was probably trained to stay calm in front of patients. But before Mark could give the scary situation much thought, Dr. Hart entered the room and things began happening at a pretty good clip.

He probably ought to slip out during the hubbub and let everyone do their job, but a particularly hard contraction struck, and Juliet's pain-filled gaze latched onto him like a drowning woman grasping for lifeline.

Mark couldn't move, couldn't leave. As if having a mind of their own, his feet slowly made their way to her bedside. "Hang on, honey. You're doing great. The baby will be here soon."

That ought to be a comfort for her, but it brought on another flurry of anxiety for Mark. Would the baby be okay? Would it have all its fingers and toes? Would they whisk it away to some baby ICU?

He didn't know how much time had passed. It didn't seem like very long to him. All he knew was that Juliet didn't appear to be hurting as bad.

"I feel like I have to push," she said.

"Hold on a minute." Dr. Hart prepared for delivery, then glanced at Mark. "Are you going to stay in here?"

"Who me?" Mark asked.

"I'd…like you…to stay," Juliet said, her voice coming out in huffs and puffs. "If you're…okay with it."

Hell, he ought to escape while he had a chance. But he'd been with her throughout this ordeal. And he'd never been one to cut out in the last ten minutes of a movie—especially one that kept the audience on the edge of their seats.

"Sure," he said. "I'll stay."

Beth Ann got on one side of Juliet and asked Mark to stand on the other. "We're going to help her push."

Help her push? What in the hell had he gotten himself into?

"I'll show you how." The nurse watched the doctor, like a runner on second looked at the third base coach.

"All right," Dr. Hart said. "Let's go."

Mark wasn't sure what was happening, but he stayed by Juliet's side, holding her legs, helping her push and strain. Before long, he could see the dark hair of a little head emerging, and his pulse surged with excitement. "Good job, honey."

About four contractions and a whole lot of pushing later, a tiny baby girl slid into the doctor's hands. She was kind of purple, and her head was misshapen—a scary mess, in Mark's opinion. He thought they ought to hide it from Juliet, but everyone was oohing and aahing, like everything was just the way it was supposed to be.

When the baby let out an angry wail, Mark realized he'd never seen a more beautiful sight. Nor one that was more precious.

"Is everything okay?" he asked, assuming that it was, since everyone continued to smile and make light of the baby's color and the shape of her head.

"They're doing fine." Dr. Hart laid the naked infant on Juliet's stomach. "Do you want to cut the cord, Mark?"

He glanced at Juliet, saw her beaming like a blessed Madonna. He couldn't very well pass on what appeared to be a special opportunity. "Sure."

The doctor handed him scissors, indicating where to cut, and Mark snipped the cord, freeing the tiny baby and making her an individual.

"Time?" Dr. Hart asked, as she continued to work on Juliet.

"Nineteen twenty-eight," another nurse said.

It was enough to make a grown man choke up. God, had he ever felt so blessed to be a part of something so special?

Beth Ann whisked the baby to a little bassinette-type bed. All the while, the little one screamed.

Mark made his way to the infant's side, just to make sure she was all right. Not that he could be of any help, but he wanted to see for himself.

After suctioning out the little mouth, Beth Ann went to work, listening to the tiny chest, among other things. Then she placed the baby on a scale. "Four pounds, eleven ounces."

Was that big enough? Mark wondered. She looked awfully tiny to him.

Beth Ann took a paper tape measure and stretched out the poor little girl, making Mark think of Popeye and Bluto tugging on Olive Oyl as they fought over her.

"Seventeen and a half inches long," Beth Ann said.

"She's petite," Dr. Hart said. "But she sounds spunky."

"Like her mother," Mark said, admiring the tiny head of thick dark hair, the button nose, the rosebud lips. What a precious little face.

He wasn't sure how long he'd stood there, marveling at the baby girl, while making sure she had just the right number of fingers and toes. But he remained long enough for the doctor to finish tending Juliet and for another nurse to put the room back in order, just like there'd never been a delivery.

A young woman with auburn hair entered the room and introduced herself to Juliet as Dr. Hodsman, a pediatrician. Then she proceeded to flip the newborn around like a rag doll, or so it seemed to Mark. He wondered if he ought to say something, tell the doctor to be more careful.

Weren't people supposed to hold a baby's head and neck? Watch out for soft spots? Not that he was an expert.

The pediatrician listened to the little girl's heart and lungs, then bent her legs at the knees and hips. The baby continued to fuss, and Mark couldn't help thinking the doctor might break a bone or pop a joint out of the socket.

"She may be nearly five weeks premature," the pediatrician said, "but her lungs are fully developed. She does have a little foot that turns in, probably because of the way she was curled up in the womb."

Something was wrong with her little foot?

Mark peered into the clear plastic bassinette where the baby lay naked, legs and arms reaching out for someone. Her mom. Or him. But no one seemed to notice.

Her right ankle turned in. Was Juliet's baby going to be crippled? Would she need surgery to correct it?

"It's nothing serious," the pediatrician said. "Her bones are soft and pliable right now. A corrective shoe will straighten it within a few months, but I don't think she'll even need that much treatment."

That was good, wasn't it?

The doctor pulled the foot. "See how easily it bends back to normal? You can work with it, helping it to bend correctly while she's eating or when you're holding her."

Mark glanced at the young mother. Even in her exhaustion, there was no denying her beauty, especially now. "The baby is beautiful, Juliet. Just like you."

"Thank you." She beamed at him, turning him inside out. "I don't know what I would have done without you, Mark."

A warm glow lit his heart, causing his chest to swell as though he'd had a hand in creating a miracle, as though he'd actually done something to bring this precious child into the world.

After the baby had a sponge bath and was bundled up like a little burrito in a flannel blanket, the nurse handed her to Juliet. "Let's try to get her to nurse."

Mark might have stayed for the birth, but he thought it would be best if he slipped out for a while now. "I'm going to get a cup of coffee before the cafeteria closes."

"You may as well get something to eat while you're there," Beth Ann said. "We're having dinner brought up to the new mommy."

"All right. I'll be back, Juliet."

After having the Salisbury steak special and a slice of chocolate cake, he savored a cup of coffee, taking time to reflect on the awesome experience he'd just had.

If Mark were a church-goer, he might whisper a

prayer of thanksgiving. But he wasn't. Still, he couldn't quell a sense of wonder, of awe.

"Hey," he whispered, his voice raspy with emotion. "Thanks. For the miracle."

Then he put his plate, cup and utensils in the plastic receptacle and headed back to maternity to tell Juliet that she'd done a great job. That she'd make a wonderful mother.

When he stepped into the birthing room, the baby was nestled in Juliet's arms. The doctor had gone, and Beth Ann was preparing a little bassinette near the hospital bed.

Mark plopped down on the chair, although he wasn't sure why. Moments later, Beth Ann left them alone.

"Are you going to stay?" Juliet asked.

He glanced up. "Here?"

"You don't have to."

Did she want him to spend the night? He tried to read her expression.

She bit on her lip, then clicked her tongue. "It's just that I was thinking about what the orderly said. About that woman trying to steal a newborn. And I know they've got security and all." She glanced at the sleeping baby in her arms. "But I'm not going to rest very well tonight. I'll keep looking at her, checking to see if she's breathing. Checking to see if she's still here."

He figured it was just a typical case of maternal anxiety. Both mother and child would be safer here than anywhere. But he wasn't going to tell Juliet she was a worrywart. Not after what she'd been through.

"I'm sure you'll both be fine. But I'll stay, if it makes you feel better. And I'll keep an eye on you both."

"Thanks." She offered him an appreciative smile. "It may sound weird, but this is the first time she hasn't really been a part of me. And it will make me feel better if you stayed."

He nodded. "You try to get some sleep. If she cries, I'll wake you."

Juliet chuckled. "If she cries, I have a feeling I'll hear her."

"Maybe so. But just in case, I'll stick around."

She stroked the little girl's cheek, then looked at Mark. "Can you lay her in the bed?"

What?

Hold her?

Well, he supposed it would be tough for Juliet to maneuver. And maybe she wasn't allowed out of bed. "Okay."

Juliet handed him the tiny bundle. The sleeping baby, still warm from her mother's embrace, felt like a bit of nothing in his arms. An empty bundle of flannel.

He tried not to spend too much time fawning over her, marveling over the healthy pink color and the way her mouth made little kissing movements, but it wasn't easy. He actually had to make himself place her in the bed.

Then, without thinking, he brushed a kiss across Juliet's brow, an affectionate gesture he hadn't planned.

It didn't seem to bother her, which he supposed was good.

"Don't worry," he told her.

"I won't." She smiled, then nestled her head into the pillow and closed her eyes.

He watched her for a while, saw her grow easy and suspected she'd fallen asleep. He'd promised to watch over her and the little one.

And he would.

He just hoped to God that he'd been right when he told her not to worry. That nothing would go wrong.

Especially on his watch.

Chapter Seven

Juliet sat up in the hospital bed, a tray of breakfast before her. Mark, bless his heart, had gone to the cafeteria. But he'd stayed with her the entire night.

He had to be exhausted, because each time she'd wakened for a feeding, he'd handed the baby to her.

She couldn't believe how helpful he'd been, how supportive. Nor could she believe how much she'd grown to appreciate having him near. Or how his smile could make her feel as though she didn't have a worry in the world when that wasn't the case. Her finances were still shaky, especially since she would need to hire a sitter after her disability ran out.

The baby whimpered, and Juliet turned to see her daughter scrunch her sweet face. Throughout the night, Mark had called her Sweet Pea, referring to the crawling infant in a Popeye cartoon. But the little girl needed a real name.

Over the past few months, Juliet had tossed around some ideas. At one time, while contemplating girls' names, she'd thought about calling the baby Manuela, after her brother. Or maybe Maria Eiena, after her *abuelita*. But before making a final decision, she'd decided to wait until her daughter arrived.

It seemed logical to make sure the baby looked like a Manuela or a Maria before dubbing her with a name that would stick for the rest of her life. And now that Juliet had seen the baby and fallen in love with her, neither seemed to fit.

But around two o'clock in the morning, she'd gotten another idea. Something that felt more appropriate and more fitting.

The door swung open, as Mark entered the room. He carried a newspaper and a disposable cup she assumed was coffee.

"Looks like Sweet Pea is giving you a chance to eat breakfast in peace," he said.

Juliet smiled and glanced at the precious little one lying in the bassinette. "So far so good, but I think she's starting to wake up now."

He made his way to the baby's bedside and studied her while she squirmed. "What are you going to call her?"

Juliet didn't respond until his gaze caught hers. "I'd like to name her after you, Mark. What do you think of Marissa?"

His eyes widened, and his lips parted. "You're going to name her after *me*?"

He seemed genuinely touched, and she was glad. "I'm not sure how I would have managed without you this past week."

Before he could respond further, a blond candy striper popped her head in the door. "Are you finished with breakfast?"

"Yes," Juliet said, taking one last sip of milk.

The bright-eyed teen crossed the room with a spring in her step and picked up Juliet's tray. "Did you hear the news?"

Mark, who'd managed to doff the sentiment from his expression the minute the candy striper entered the room, slipped into reporter mode. "What news?"

"A couple of guys hunting for gold near Turner Grade found several large nuggets. They showed the E.R. staff, and everyone said they were the biggest ones yet." The teenager smiled, revealing a set of rainbow-colored braces. "My grandpa left us a piece of property that used to be a gold mine in the olden days. And my dad is going to get a second mortgage on our house so he can buy the equipment and hire a crew to start working it again."

Juliet glanced at Mark, knowing what he was thinking—that the poor candy striper's father was wasting his time, as well as risking the family's financial security.

Mark didn't comment, didn't deflate the young woman's hope, which was good. And Juliet, who always tried to keep a positive outlook, was glad he'd held his tongue. But she had to admit even she found the man's enthusiasm a bit scary. After all, Mark had been right about something. Most of the gold hunters would end up empty-handed.

"What were the prospectors doing in the E.R.?" Mark asked.

"Apparently, they'd been celebrating their find at The Hitching Post last night. On the way to the parking lot, one of them tripped and cut his hand on a bottle of beer he'd been holding. So he came in for stitches."

"Crazy fools." Mark glanced at Juliet, with a see-what-I-mean look in his eye, which silently pointed out the downside of the gold rush.

It was amazing. Juliet and Mark had actually communicated in a look, a glance. Just like married couples seemed to do.

For a moment, she wondered what had happened between them in the past week. What had changed? Had they forged some kind of a bond? And if so, what direction would their friendship take?

But rather than get carried away, she shrugged off her question, deciding to take one day at a time.

"The E.R. gets a lot of gold-rush related injuries," Mark said.

"They sure do." The candy striper grinned. "Just this morning, someone came in with a gunshot wound."

"That's a lot more serious than a cut or broken bone," Mark said. "Was it another prospector?"

"Uh-huh. My friend is a nurse's aide, and she told

me it was a property dispute or something like that."
The teenager lifted Juliet's tray. "Well, I'd better get
back to work." Then she left the room and went on her
way.

Juliet glanced at Mark, saw his furrowed brow.

Was he contemplating the value of the candy striper's gossip? Or the importance of the land dispute?

"It looks like your story is taking off without you,"
Juliet said. "Marissa and I are doing okay. Why don't
you take some time to yourself?"

"Maybe I will." He glanced at the baby, watched
her squirm and fuss. "Mind if I pick her up? I think
she's hungry."

Juliet could just as easily take care of the baby herself, but she had a feeling Mark liked being helpful.
"Please do."

He held the child against his chest for a bit longer
than necessary, which Juliet thought was sweet. That
fish-out-of-water expression hadn't completely disap-
peared, but he'd grown more confident.

"Have a nice breakfast, Sweet Pea." He ran a knuc-
kle along the baby's cheek, then handed her to Juliet.
"I'll be back later this afternoon."

"That's fine. Dr. Hart was just here. She wants to
keep us at least another night, just to make sure Marissa is nursing well and doesn't develop any problems
related to her premature birth."

"Ma-ris-sa," he said, enunciating each sound. His
eyes lit up, as he smiled. "I'm not sure if I told you,
but I like that. It's a pretty name for a pretty little
girl."

Then he grabbed his coffee, rolled up the newspaper and headed for the door. Off to work. Just like a typical new father.

Stop that, Juliet told herself. *Soy la tonta del barrio,* the biggest fool in town.

Mark had been a good friend—that's all. And she couldn't let those kinds of silly thoughts take root.

Lord knew she didn't need to set herself up for any more disappointments in her life.

The newspaper office was located along South Main, just a few blocks from Town Square. It wasn't a big building, but then again, the *Thunder Canyon Nugget* was only a weekly.

Mark had come by twice before, not long after he'd arrived in town. But the publisher and editor, Roy Canfield, had an Out To Lunch sign on the door. And the sign had remained there all afternoon.

But today Mark was in luck—no sign and the door of the white-stucco building was unlocked.

He entered the small front office and caught the heady scent of newsprint and ink.

A heavyset, salt-and-pepper-haired man in a tweed sports jacket sat at a desk near a door leading to the back. His leather desk chair squeaked as he turned from his work. "Can I help you?"

"My name's Mark Anderson. I'm with Golden Eagle News Service. Are you Mr. Canfield?"

"Yes, siree." The sixty-something man stood and reached out a hand in greeting. "But call me Roy."

They shook hands, and Mark cut to the chase. "I

read your latest editorial. In fact, I was a bit surprised that it was so well-written and thought-provoking."

"Because you agree with me? Or because the *Nugget* is just a weekly?" Roy crossed his arms above an ample belly, but his smile indicated he hadn't found the comment offensive.

Mark returned his smile. "Actually, I disagreed with you. And I plan to write a letter in rebuttal."

"Good!" Roy stood as tall as his five-and-a-half foot frame would allow, putting quite a strain on his red suspenders. "I'm always up for a heated debate."

Mark smiled. "I must admit the issue I read was better than I expected."

"I bought the *Nugget* two years ago, after I retired from a big-city press. And I've tried to make it a quality newspaper while maintaining the small-town appeal."

"You've done a good job. I expected to see something about a two-headed cow or a fifty-pound rutabaga."

"That's what I've tried to get away from ever since I bought this rag." Roy's blue eyes glistened. "It's not always easy to find real news in a small town. Do you know what the last editor ran on the front page the day before I took the helm?"

Mark shook his head. "Hard telling."

Roy chuckled, his belly shaking with mirth. "Elmer Godwin, who was suffering from a godawful case of gout, got drunk and, in his frustration over the pain, tried to cut off his big toe and damn near bled to death."

A wry smile tugged at Mark's lips. "Sorry I missed that issue."

"*That Golden Eagle* would have paid you plenty for a newsflash like that." Roy indicated a chair in front of his desk. "Why don't you take a seat? It isn't often we get a hotshot reporter from the city in town."

There was something about Roy Canfield that Mark liked, that he could relate to, although he sure as hell didn't know what it was. The fact that they were both journalists, he supposed.

"I've been sent to write a big spread on the gold rush," Mark told the older man. "But I doubt there's anything worthy of a story."

"You gotta believe, son." Canfield's blue eyes sparkled.

"Come on, Roy." Mark took the seat across from the heavyset older man. "The fortune hunters are spitting into the wind."

"What about those two brothers who found themselves a couple of good-size nuggets yesterday?"

"You mean the two guys who celebrated at The Hitching Post and ended up at the E.R. getting stitches in one of their hands?" Mark clucked his tongue. "Sure, there might be a few nuggets out there. But the real story lies in the broken dreams of those foolish enough to sell their homes and buy prospecting gear, especially when they don't know squat about mining gold."

"You know who Caleb Douglas is?" Canfield asked.

"Yeah. He's a wealthy businessman and cattle baron who's developing that new ski resort."

Canfield nodded. "And right now, the man is more interested in finding the deed to the Queen of Hearts mine."

"I'd heard he was still having trouble locating the deed. Are you saying he's caught gold fever?"

"For years, that boarded up mine was considered worthless, except as a piece of real estate. And more recently, as you probably know, Caleb has been focused on that fancy new ski resort and the ground-breaking ceremony next month. But that's not the case anymore." Canfield leaned back in his chair, leather creaking and wood squeaking as he rocked. "When a couple of squatters began to hunt for gold on Caleb's property, he was concerned about liability, more than anything else. After all, enough of those foolish gold hunters have already ended up at the Thunder Canyon E.R. So he posted No Trespassing signs."

"Makes sense. Besides, any gold on the property belongs to him."

"But now, Caleb realizes that just because the Queen of Hearts played out years ago doesn't mean there's not a new vein."

"Okay," Mark said. "Let's say there is still gold in the Queen of Hearts. How's that going to help all those prospectors combing the hills?"

"It won't. But that's not where your story is, son."

"What do you mean?"

"Yesterday, a squatter challenged Caleb, spouting rumors about mine ownership and questioning who actually had the legal right to run off anyone from the property." Roy leaned forward, resting his elbows on the desk. "If you've kept your ears open, you know there are a lot of rumors about how old Amos Douglas won the Queen of Hearts in a poker game a century or more ago. And there's a lesser known story that some prospector won it back."

"I went to high school in Thunder Canyon, even though I haven't been back in twenty years. So I'm familiar with the rumors. You think there's anything to them?"

Roy shrugged, reached for a pencil and twiddled it through his fingers. "Who knows? Caleb hadn't been able to find the deed before, thinking it just wasn't handy. But since then, he began to hunt diligently, and so far, he's come up empty-handed."

"How about a title search down at the courthouse?"

"He's having trouble with that, too. Especially with Harvey Watson out of town on vacation."

Watson, Mark realized, was the clerk who was trying to computerize the old ledgers.

The semiretired journalist chuckled. "You look bumfuzzled. If I were still at the *Tribune,* I'd probably scoop you on this one. But I'm not."

"What are you thinking?" Mark asked, finding himself interested in the old man's take on the situation.

"If Caleb can't find the deed, it makes me think at least one of those old rumors must be true. That Amos sold off the property, thinking it was worthless. Or that he lost it in a card game. Or that it was stolen out from under his nose." The editor grinned like a cat in an aviary. "And that's where your story is, son."

Mark pondered what the older man had said. And he found his interest stimulated. Maybe Canfield was right. Maybe Caleb Douglas didn't own the property. And if there was a new vein, someone else stood to profit. Someone who might not realize it.

"Well," Roy said, getting to his feet. "I hate to rush you. But I've got to run home and eat lunch. My wife has been on my case. She hates every minute I spend down here, although I think she's more resentful of the money I invested. But what the hell would I do with my time if I retired completely?"

Mark sure didn't know what to tell him.

"The smell of ink is in my blood. I love my work. And I can't see myself on one of those Caribbean cruises she's been pestering me to take, even if I could find the time. I finally got her to take one with her sister, Mildred."

Canfield didn't need to explain. Mark understood how the newspaper got in a man's blood. And how a woman could get upset about the time a man spent away from home.

Hell, Mark had a divorce decree to prove it.

His marriage to Susan, of course, had been years ago. And it hadn't lasted very long. Just long enough for him to learn how unhappy his travels had made a woman whose only goal in life was to create a home and be a mother—until she got fed up and threw it all away.

But that was all right. Mark loved his job, and having a family would have only tied him down.

As he followed Roy to the door, his thoughts

drifted to Juliet and the baby, although he wasn't sure why. Because they'd spent so much time together, he supposed. Because he probably ought to check on them and make sure things were still okay.

"By the way," Roy said, as he flipped over the Out To Lunch sign and locked the door. "Are you the reporter who's been looking after the pregnant waitress at The Hitching Post?"

"Yeah. News travels fast."

"Hey, Thunder Canyon news is my business, even if it isn't Pulitzer material." Roy grinned. "So, did that pretty young woman have her baby?"

"Yeah," Mark said, a warm glow building in his chest. "Juliet had a tiny little girl. Four pounds, eleven ounces."

The older man blew out a whistle. "That's small. Mother and baby doing well?"

"Yeah. They're doing great."

"What'd Juliet name the child?" the editor asked. "I might write up a little blurb for the paper."

"Marissa."

"Pretty name."

"Thanks," Mark said, wondering why he'd felt as though he'd been given a compliment.

Juliet and Marissa stayed in the hospital for two nights and most of the next day. After promising to make an appointment for the baby to see a pediatrician for a weight check in three days, they were released around dinnertime, and Mark took them home.

Then, while mother and baby settled in, Mark went

downstairs and purchased dinner at The Hitching Post, even though he was a bit sick of their meals.

He returned to the apartment and let himself in.

"It's me," he said, setting the bags of food on the table.

"I'm in here," Juliet called from the bedroom.

He entered and found her placing the baby in a secondhand cradle and covering her with a green crocheted blanket. He wondered if she'd brought the cradle from San Diego, but didn't ask. He was too caught up in the scene before him.

Juliet wore a white cotton nightgown, the thin material and the lamplight allowing him a glimpse of her silhouette. The way her breasts seemed fuller, the nipples pronounced. Her belly hadn't gone back to its normal size, yet she looked beautiful standing over the baby's bed, her hair glossy and hanging free.

He scoffed at himself for staring. And for finding her still attractive. "I...uh...got pot roast this evening. And strawberry shortcake for dessert."

"Thanks. That sounds delicious." She cast him a smile, one that lit her face and made him realize how pretty she was without makeup and any special effects.

He raked a hand through his hair and leaned against the doorjamb. "Mrs. Tasker sent up a bottle of sparkling apple cider in celebration."

"That was nice of her."

"She'd also like to come up and see the baby, but I told her tonight wasn't a good time." Actually, he didn't like the idea of having people breathe over the baby. Not yet. She was too tiny, too vulnerable. What if Marissa caught a germ and got sick?

"I'm a bit tired," Juliet admitted. "Tomorrow would be better."

Mark hoped she didn't think he was moving in, or something. He had every intention of taking his shaving kit back to the inn and staying where he belonged

"If you don't mind, I'll join you for dinner. Then I'll head back to the inn."

"All right." Her smile faltered, waned. Was she disappointed that he'd be leaving? Afraid she couldn't handle the baby alone yet?

"Unless you'd rather I stayed one more night," he added.

"No, that's all right. I think we'll be fine." She tucked a strand of hair behind her ear, then glanced at Marissa's sleeping form. "Give me a minute, and I'll be right there."

He nodded, then returned to the dining area. Moments later, she joined him. But she'd slipped on her blue robe and a pair of scruffy white slippers.

Was she getting shy all of a sudden? Or just chilled?

"Should I turn up the heat?" he asked.

"No, I'm not cold."

Okay. So she wasn't wearing the robe to ward off a chill. But Mark let it drop.

They ate dinner in silence, an awkwardness settling over them. Mark didn't have a clue what had caused it. Not exactly. The fact that they'd been playing house maybe. That they'd been a couple for nearly a week. And now playtime was over.

He opened the bottle of sparkling cider and poured them both a glass. Lifting his, he said, "To Marissa."

Juliet clinked her glass against his, then took a sip. He watched the movement of her swallow, admired the shape of her neck, as he had before. Swanlike. Pretty.

She stood and moved toward the bookshelf that held her family photos, then picked one up, communing with her family the only way she could. She lifted another silver frame, then swiped a hand under her eyes. Her shoulders trembled.

Oh, hell. She was crying.

His mind told him to stay seated. To let her grieve alone. To mind his own business. To find a reason to leave. But for some inexplicable reason, he stood and made his way to her side.

"Are you okay?" he asked.

She turned, eyes red and watery. A tear slid down her face. "I'm so sorry they couldn't see Marissa. That they can't be a part of her life."

Mark wrapped her in his arms and drew her close, breathing in the citrusy scent of her shampoo. Offering her his strength. Hoping his embrace was enough.

Her tears continued to fall, so he continued to hold her.

"I'm really sorry," she whispered into his cotton dress shirt, making it warm and moist. "I haven't done this in a long time."

"It's the baby. And hormones," he said, although he had no idea if that were true. It sounded reasonable, he supposed.

His mother used to say that to Kelly, when she locked herself in her room for days at a time. Mark had always figured his sister was depressed because the JOB she'd married had left her barefoot and pregnant. But his parents had been too busy to seek help for her, counseling. Something.

"You're probably right," Juliet said, causing him to wonder what it was that he'd said. "It's normal to have some depression after birth. Some people call it the baby blues."

She sniffled, as if the crying jag were all over.

Whew. This childbirth stuff was so new. So out of his league.

As he loosened his embrace and let her go, she glanced at the bookshelf, ran her hand along a watermark on the wood. "Manny made that stain. He…"

She sniffled again, then batted away a new tear. And then another.

The next thing Mark knew, he was holding her again. And she was trembling in his arms. "Come on, honey. Let's take a walk into the other room."

Of course, the only other room was the bedroom, where Marissa slept. This apartment was so damn small there was no escape from the memories of the past. But maybe the baby would offer her a promise of the future.

When they reached the bed, he used his thumbs to wipe the tears from her eyes. "Why don't you lie down? You ought to rest while the baby is sleeping."

"Will you lie down with me? Just for a minute or two?"

He nodded, willing to do anything to make her feel better. To see that pretty Pollyanna smile again.

"Sure." He joined her on the bed, fully clothed, his loafers still on his feet.

He tried his best to comfort her, as they lay there for the longest time, not talking. Not needing to.

When she finally fell asleep, he continued to hold her.

And he didn't have the foggiest idea why.

Chapter Eight

Juliet slept better than she had in years.

She'd missed human contact, the warmth of a touch, the comfort of an embrace, the steady beat of a heart. So she nestled in a sweet dimension, somewhere between dreamland and reality, relishing a peaceful slumber.

Until Marissa fussed and began to root into the sheets of her cradle.

Juliet opened her eyes, ready to reach for her daughter and feed her. But she couldn't move.

Mark had one arm under her neck and the other around her waist, holding her close.

They'd left a lamp on in the other room, which allowed her to see, and she sought the lighted dial of the clock on the dresser.

Almost midnight.

They'd lain like that for nearly three hours, like lovers. Like husband and wife. New parents.

For just a moment, she let herself go, let herself pretend that Mark loved her, that she loved him in return. And that her daughter had a devoted family in which she could grow up.

But love was a game of pretend Juliet didn't dare play.

"Mark," she whispered softly.

He grunted, then drew her closer. His chin nestled in her hair, the faint mountain-fresh scent of his cologne riding gently in the night air.

"Mark," she said again, this time louder. "I need to feed the baby."

"Huh?"

Marissa let out a cry, and the poor guy nearly jumped through the ceiling.

The mattress wobbled as he braced himself on an elbow and scanned the room. "God, I'm so sorry. I fell asleep. I must have been more tired than I realized."

Juliet smiled, as she climbed from bed and retrieved her hungry daughter. "That's okay."

He glanced at the clock and blew out a sigh. "I guess it's too late to go back to the inn. But I... uh...can go out to the sofa."

She smiled at his sheepish expression, at his thoughtfulness. "Don't bother. Go on back to sleep."

"Are you sure?" He sat on the mattress and glanced at the single loafer he wore, probably wondering where he'd kicked off the other one.

"I'm not sure what's happened between us," she said, as she shushed Marissa. "But it's pretty safe to say we've become close friends in the past week or so."

He raked a hand through his sleep-tousled hair. "I guess you're right."

"So if you don't mind if I nurse her, I don't mind if you're in the same room. After all, you've seen me at my worst."

He kicked off his remaining shoe, which thumped onto the floor, then laid back down, on top of the comforter, and rested his head on the pillow.

As Marissa cried, anxious to eat, Juliet unbuttoned the front of her gown, releasing a breast and offering it to her child. Within moments, the baby latched on. Juliet's milk was just starting to come in—at least she suspected it was. Her breasts were fuller, and Marissa seemed to be swallowing more than she had before.

The lamplight from the living room cast a dull glow through the bedroom door, making it easy to see, easy to marvel at her pretty, dark-haired baby.

Juliet looked over her shoulder, saw Mark lying in bed, eyes open, watching her. She wasn't sure there was much to see, other than an outline of her breast. And interestingly enough, she didn't feel shy or embarrassed.

She felt womanly.

"Do you want me to get you anything?" he asked. "A diaper or a glass of water?"

She offered him a smile that came from her heart. "How did I ever get by without a friend like you?"

He didn't answer. And that was just as well, because the underlying reality echoed in her mind.

Once Mark was gone, she'd have to get by on her own again.

Ever since Mark had fallen asleep with Juliet and wakened with her in his arms, he'd gone back to the Wander-On-Inn each night at bedtime.

In the past, he'd always enjoyed the quiet hours before turning in. But lately, he worried about what was going on at the apartment across the street, about whether Juliet was okay, whether the baby was sleeping longer between feedings.

He supposed Juliet had been right about their friendship. They'd definitely forged some kind of a bond in the past two weeks. A bond that was just as frightening as it was appealing.

Somehow, the pretty young mother had touched his heart—as a friend, of course. And her daughter had done the same thing.

So that was why, a week after Marissa was born, Mark drove Juliet and the baby to the clinic for a weight check.

Juliet had said she could probably drive herself, since she'd had an easy birth and hadn't needed any medication or an episiotomy. But Mark had still insisted on going. To be honest, he wanted to make sure that Marissa was gaining weight and that everything was all right.

He secured the car seat in the back of his rented sedan, while Juliet carried the baby down the steps.

And moments later, they were on their way to the Lone Pine Medical Building, which was located on White Water Drive, just past the entrance to the hospital.

Several different doctors, including Doc Emerson, Juliet's primary physician, housed their offices in a single building that shared a large, single waiting room. A registration desk sat in each open doorway. They signed in at the pediatrician's office and took a seat near the entry.

Their appointment wasn't supposed to take long, since it was with the nurse and not a full-blown checkup.

About ten minutes after they signed in at the pediatric desk, a grandmotherly blonde wearing a blue smock with a Noah's ark print called Marissa's name.

"I'm Karen," she said, as she led them back to a small exam room.

Juliet was asked to undress the sleeping baby— something Marissa didn't like. Her wail of protest soon filled the air.

Karen placed the naked, crying baby on the scale and fiddled with the dial. "There we go. Four pounds, eleven and a half ounces."

Uh-oh. Only a half ounce? That wasn't very much, was it? At this rate, Marissa would be in kindergarten before she hit the ten-pound mark.

"Good job, Mom." Karen picked up the unhappy baby and handed her to Juliet. "She's already regained her birth weight."

"That's good," Juliet said. "She'd dropped down to four pounds, six ounces when we left the hospital."

Oh. So she was making up for lost weight. Mark blew out a sigh. "When do we have to bring her back in?"

The "we" slipped out without him realizing it.

Damn, he was going to have to step back and let Juliet and Marissa get on with their lives. He'd be leaving town shortly—just as soon as he finished the story.

"Since the baby was a good four weeks early and small," the nurse said, "we'd like to see her in another week. But so far, so good. She's doing just great. Do you have any questions?"

"When can she take a bath?" Juliet asked.

"The cord is just dangling. So as soon as it falls off, you can bathe her."

Mark didn't like the thought of the tiny girl in the bathtub. "Isn't she too little for the tub?"

The nurse smiled. "If you don't have one of those plastic baby baths, you can bathe her in the kitchen sink."

"Oh," he said. There was a lot about babies he still didn't know.

The nurse led them to the desk where they could make an appointment. When they settled on next Friday at two, the receptionist said, "There's a ten-dollar co-pay for this visit."

Mark reached for his wallet.

"What are you doing?" Juliet tugged at his shirt-sleeve. "I can pay that."

"I know." But he wasn't going to let her. She had a lot of upcoming expenses—a babysitter, for one. He whipped out a twenty. "Let me take care of this."

The woman at the desk gave him change and they returned to the car. All the while, Marissa made quite a racket, and no amount of shushing or gentle swaying seemed to help.

"Do you mind if I feed her first?" Juliet asked.

"No. Go ahead." Mark hadn't meant to watch, to see her unbutton her pink cotton blouse and offer a breast to the child. But he couldn't turn away.

It's not as though there was anything sexual about it. Well, not really. But the attraction, the appeal, was just as strong, just as powerful.

For a moment, he wondered if he would ever be part of a family—like this one. But he quickly shook off the crazy notion.

After all, he'd *been* married once. To a pretty coed he'd met in college, a homebody with a teaching credential. The kind of woman who wanted to be a mother and create a family. A sweet, twenty-two-year-old redhead who'd morphed into a whiny nag after the first six months. And then she'd offered him an ultimatum—either his marriage or his career.

Mark had told her that he couldn't walk away from the job he loved, especially not while on an assignment. And when he got back to town, she was gone—along with the furniture and all the wedding gifts.

The failure of the marriage had hurt, even though he'd sensed it coming. But he hadn't fought the divorce, letting his ex have all the stuff they'd acquired in the short time they'd been together.

What the hell. He would have had to put everything in storage anyway.

After Marissa had been burped and placed into the car seat, Mark headed home along White Water Drive.

The sky was a vast, springtime blue, and the sun promised to warm the wintry chill in the breeze and carry them to summer. Yet Mark had learned the weather in Montana could turn stormy on Mother Nature's whim.

As they neared the colorful flags that lined the entrance of Ranch View Estates, a hell of an idea began to form.

Mark's accountant had been after him for years to buy a home—as an investment, as a much needed tax write-off. But Mark had dragged his feet.

Hell, he'd let the execs at Golden Eagle know that he was willing to go anywhere the company sent him. So why have a house when he was never home?

Instead, he'd socked away the cash he would have spent on a mortgage and put it into a money market account that had been growing steadily. With his globe-trotting lifestyle, complete with a hefty expense account, he didn't have much opportunity to spend his earnings.

Still, he thought about what his accountant had said.

What if he bought one of those ranch-style houses? Just a small one, of course. He could let Juliet and the baby live there, and she could take care of the property for him—in lieu of rent. After all, he'd be taxed on rental income anyway, wouldn't he?

And she certainly didn't need to be wasting money that was better spent elsewhere. Her wages and tips from The Hitching Post couldn't possibly be very much, and he suspected she would have a difficult time making ends meet, especially if she had to hire a sitter.

And speaking of babysitters, they'd better find someone good. Someone competent. Mark didn't like the idea of just anyone looking after Marissa.

"It's a pretty day," Juliet said.

"Yeah. It is." And it was too nice for her and the baby to stay cooped up in that drab old apartment. "I was planning to go by the museum today. Would you and Marissa like to go with me?"

"Sure. We'd love to. On my days off, I used to spend a lot of time there." She crossed her arms and slid him a questioning look. "But why do *you* want to go to the museum? I thought history didn't interest you."

"Normally, it wouldn't. But I'm looking for information about the Queen of Hearts that will add a little color and flavor the article I'm writing. And while I interview the docent, you and Marissa can wander around and enjoy the place all you want."

"We will." Then she flashed him a pretty smile that turned him every which way but loose.

Damn. He was growing a little too fond of the mother and her baby. Too concerned about their welfare.

It was definitely time to finish his story and get the hell out of Dodge.

The Thunder Canyon Museum was located on two acres of land on Elm Street, in a barn-red clapboard structure that had been a schoolhouse in the late eighteen hundreds. Originally, it had been built in the classic, one-room style, with a foyer/mudroom and big closet in front, the schoolroom in the center and a kitchen/workroom in back.

But over the years, outbuildings had been added until the community outgrew the facility. And when the new schools were built on the other side of town, the historical society had taken over the original structure and created a museum.

From what Juliet understood, townspeople had donated money and different artifacts over the years, which allowed the museum to include various exhibits that showed how the early settlers lived. And the biggest contributor had been Caleb Douglas.

There was also a roped-off area that displayed clothing, accessories and toiletries that once belonged to Lily Divine, the Shady Lady.

Juliet had always found that particular display to be the most interesting. Or maybe it was the woman's occupation as a saloon owner and possibly a madam that set her curiosity soaring. She wished she could have met Lily. And that she could have lived in the late nineteenth century.

That period in history had always fascinated her, which was why she'd spent so much time at the old schoolhouse museum.

And on each visit, she'd enjoyed her many chats with the various docents, all volunteers and members of the Thunder Canyon Historical Society. In fact, she'd even thought about joining the interesting group.

As Mark parked the sedan on the side of the building, Juliet spotted the old shed-style barn in back. It didn't look like much now, but on her last visit one of the docents had mentioned a plan to make it into a blacksmith exhibit. Juliet thought it would make a nice addition.

She got out of the car, and as she opened the passenger door to take Marissa from the car seat, a soprano voice sang out.

"Yoo-hoo! Mark Anderson, is that you?" A heavy-set woman in a yellow, floral-printed dress wiggled her fingers in greeting.

Mark made his way toward the smiling matron. "Yeah. It's me, Mrs. Eagleston."

"Why look at you. All grown up. Of course, I would have known you anywhere, even if your mother hadn't told me you'd come into town on that big assignment. She's so proud of you."

"You're looking well, Mrs. Eagleston."

"Well, thank you, Mark." She fingered the side of her lacquered hairdo, where mousy-colored strands had been swept into a beehive. "But after all these years, you'll have to drop the formality and call me Gladys."

Mark smiled, yet his iceberg stance convinced Juliet that he wasn't happy about seeing his mother's friend.

Juliet pulled Marissa from the car seat and adjusted the blanket, blocking the sunshine and the cool breeze from her face.

"I'll bet your folks were tickled pink to see you," the older woman said.

Mark didn't respond.

Because he had yet to visit them, Juliet suspected. And apparently, the Andersons hadn't told their friend that he hadn't. Were they all pretending that a falling-out hadn't occurred? That everything was fine? And that their family interactions were normal?

"I hope that new medication helps your father's arthritis. It's a shame that he's had to quit bowling. He and your mother used to enjoy the Wednesday evening Gutter Busters. And I gotta tell you, we all miss them. Jess and Anne-Marie were a hoot to bowl with. Of course, they still come watch. But it's not quite the same."

Mark maintained a detached smile.

Juliet wondered if Gladys knew about the family rift, if she'd noticed the lack of warmth and affection in Mark's voice or if she suspected his discomfort when talking about his parents.

It broke Juliet's heart to think Mark was going to allow that estrangement to continue. Especially when she'd give anything to have her family back.

Mark didn't appear to appreciate what he had— two parents, Jess and Anne-Marie Anderson, owners of the Big Sky Motel. A couple who enjoyed bowling on Wednesday nights, a man and woman whose friends thought they were a hoot.

Had Mark even known that his mother was proud of him? Or that his father suffered with arthritis?

"Well, it was good to see you, Gladys." Mark placed a hand on Juliet's shoulder. "But we'd better get the baby inside."

"The baby?" The older woman brightened and edged closer to Marissa. "Oooh. Can I take a little peek?"

"Of course." Juliet unfolded the blanket to reveal her daughter's face.

"Well, bless my soul. What a beautiful baby. And such a tiny one. A preemie, it looks like. How much does she weigh?"

"Four pounds, eleven and a half ounces," Mark said. "And we really ought to get her inside. It's a bit breezy out here."

"Of course." Gladys studied Juliet. "I'm afraid I haven't met your wife, yet."

Mark's hand, which had warmed Juliet's shoulder, dropped to his side. "She isn't my wife. This is Juliet Rivera. A friend."

"Oh," Gladys said, her eyes growing wide. "You're the waitress at The Hitching Post, aren't you?"

Juliet nodded.

"It's nice to meet you dear." The breeze whipped a strand of hair from Gladys's upsweep, and she batted it away. "For a moment, I thought I'd have to get after Anne-Marie for not telling me she was finally a grandma."

Mark threw back his shoulders like a Buckingham guard with hemorrhoids. "Take care, Gladys." Then he ushered Juliet and the baby out of the parking lot and to the museum.

Juliet opened her mouth to complain, to tell Mark that he could have been nicer to the lady, but she bit her tongue, deciding to put some thought into her comments, especially since she intended to help him mend fences.

Mark had made his parents sound like ogres. But after listening to Gladys, that hardly seemed the case.

Juliet would do whatever she could to help him make things right. After all, it was the least she could do. Mark had proven to be a good friend.

A very special friend.

Or was it more than that?

The kiss they'd shared crossed her mind, as did the night he'd slept by her side, arms holding her as though they'd become much more than friends. But as pleasant as that thought was, she shoved the possibility aside.

The kiss as well as the embrace had only happened once.

Mark hadn't ever kissed her again. And the morning after they'd slept together in her bed, he'd moved back to the Wander-On Inn as soon as the sun rose.

No, Mark wasn't into families and commitments. He loved his job and traveling on assignment. And he'd made no secret that once his work was through he'd leave Thunder Canyon for good.

Before long, he'd leave Juliet behind.

Just as he'd left Jess and Anne-Marie Anderson.

Chapter Nine

As Mark and Juliet entered the building through the front door and stepped into a reception area that had once been the old mudroom, he caught a musty whiff of worn fabric, old paper and faded memories.

They continued to the central part of the museum, which had been the original schoolroom. The windows had been closed up and walled over. And two rooms had been added to each side.

Through the open doorway on the left, Mark could see a display of gold panning equipment and what looked like Native American relics.

He ought to head for the gold mine and prospecting display, but his feet didn't move. Instead, he studied Juliet.

With the baby in her arms, she moved slowly

through the room, browsing various display cases and wearing a smile that only a history buff could appreciate—or a man who found the beautiful young woman intriguing.

Mark might not share her interest in antiques and dusty exhibits of outdated memorabilia, but he enjoyed watching her run a hand lovingly over a glass case, seeing interest light her eyes.

"Folks, I'll be with you in a minute," a man's voice called from the back. A familiar voice?

"All right," Juliet responded. "We'll make ourselves at home, Ben."

Ben Saunders?

Mark's old high school teacher? Now there was a *real* history nut. And just the guy Mark needed to talk to.

"Why, Juliet Rivera," Mr. Saunders said, making his way from the back room to the center of the museum. "I didn't expect to see you so soon after your baby's birth. The last time I stopped by The Hitching Post, Martha Tasker told me you had a little girl and were on maternity leave."

Obviously, Juliet hadn't been kidding about spending a lot of time in Old Town. And at the museum.

"Did you bring that little baby to get her first taste of Thunder Canyon history?" Mr. Saunders asked.

"I sure did." Juliet cast a loving smile on the baby she held in her arms. "But she'll probably sleep through it."

Mr. Saunders laughed, still unaware that Mark was in the room, and peered at Marissa. "I heard she was a few weeks premature, but I had no idea she was so small. Or that she was just as pretty as her mama."

Ben Saunders hadn't changed much, Mark decided, even though the former high school teacher was probably pushing seventy. He'd grown a bit heavier, and his hair had turned white. But he seemed just as friendly with those who shared his interest in history.

In the classroom, Mark hadn't been one of them.

When Saunders finally scanned the room and spotted Mark, recognition flashed in his eyes. "Why if it isn't one of my old students. Mark Anderson. The cocky kid who used to sit in the back row and shoot spitballs when I wasn't looking."

Mark grinned. He'd never been caught in the act. But he'd had a feeling Mr. Saunders had figured out who the culprit had been. "How do you do, sir?"

As they shook hands, Mr. Saunders beamed. "You know, it didn't surprise me when I heard you became a reporter."

"Why's that?" Mark asked.

"You wrote a heck of a paper on the devastating effects gold rushes have had on some people, especially the Indians and the Chinese. It was more like an exposé than a report. And I knew you had real talent putting your thoughts into words."

So, his former history teacher had remembered his work. Mark couldn't help a soaring sense of pride in a ten-page paper he'd thrown out years ago. "I'll admit full responsibility for the paper, sir. But not the spit-wads. I can't remember anyone in my class doing something so tacky and disrespectful."

"Well, I can. Sometimes I'd go home and find one stuck in my hair." Mr. Saunders chuckled. "Would you like a private tour of the museum? Or do you want to wander around on your own?"

"Juliet may want to wander, but I'd like the tour. I have some questions I'd like to ask you about the Queen of Hearts."

"I'll tag along, too," Juliet said, holding the sleeping baby in the crook of her arm. "It's always so interesting when you share those tidbits of Thunder Canyon history."

"Great." Mr. Saunders took them through the museum, stopping at each roped off section. They saw a typical parlor, the replicated interior of a one-room pioneer home and a fancy bedroom suite made out of mahogany, complete with a heavy, four-poster bed, matching bureaus, chairs and a vanity. A velvet patchwork quilt covered the mattress.

"This bedroom set was donated by the Douglas family," Ben said. "Notice the fine workmanship, the detail in the pineapple finials."

"It's beautiful." Juliet stroked the grain of the wood.

"This furniture belonged to Amos and Catherine Douglas," the older man added. "And it once graced a guestroom at the Lazy D."

Mark paused, not ready to move on. "Speaking of Amos Douglas, how did he really acquire the Queen of Hearts?"

"Well," Ben said. "There are several legends, none of which has been proven. Most people believe Amos won the property in a poker game from a prospector with a drinking problem."

"And what about you?"

Ben smiled. "I favor the story about him winning it from a renegade outlaw."

That one was new to Mark. "Which outlaw?"

"A redheaded fellow folks claimed was as crazy as a patchwork quilt." Ben chuckled. "Of course, in this day and age, we'd probably say he suffered from post-traumatic stress syndrome, caused by cruelties of the Civil War."

Mark's interest piqued. "Tell me about him."

"Crazy Red Phelps was once a Confederate soldier who fought alongside the Rafferty brothers, a couple of natural born hell-raisers who didn't care whether the war was over or not. They formed a ragtag outfit of renegade soldiers and vigilantes, but that didn't last long. They soon moved on to robbing trains and banks in Colorado."

"I've heard of the Rafferty gang," Juliet said. "They weren't as big or well known as Frank and Jesse James or the Daltons, but they did their share of robbing and killing."

"That's right." Ben tugged at the waistband of his slacks. "Crazy Red and Bobby Joe Rafferty, the head of the gang, fell for the same woman, a widow named Sally McKenzie who ran a stage stop about fifty miles outside of Denver. The fight over the woman created some bad blood between the two, and a shoot-out resulted."

"Who won?"

"Sally, if you ask me." Ben chuckled. "When Crazy Red shot Billy Joe between the eyes, she pulled out her shotgun and blasted Crazy Red in the shoulder, then ran him off. He went on to pull a few armed robberies by himself and eventually ended up in Thunder Canyon, looking for gold and a piece of the action."

"And you think Crazy Red got a hold of the Queen of Hearts?" Mark asked.

"An old newspaper quoted Crazy Red as claiming the mine rightfully belonged to him. And that he meant to have it, one way or another."

"And you believe the claim of a thief who'd been dubbed with the nickname of Crazy?"

"Nope. But he was the kind of man who might have stolen the deed." Ben slipped his hands into the pockets of his gray dress slacks. "And that could explain why Caleb Douglas can't find it."

Before Mark could respond, the telephone rang.

"Excuse me," Ben said. "I need to answer that."

Juliet, who held Marissa with one arm, tugged at Mark's shirtsleeve, a habit that always amazed him. Why didn't she just grab his hand or touch him?

"I want to show you something." She led him to the small room with the Shady Lady display and pointed to a tall case that held a mannequin wearing a faded red satin dress with a scooped neckline and trimmed with black lace. "That dress belonged to Lily Divine, the original owner of the Shady Lady saloon."

Several ropes of fake pearls looped around the

mannequin's neck, and a big black ostrich feather adorned the fake hair.

"I like the black fan the mannequin is holding," Juliet added. "See the workmanship? It's edged with chantilly lace and a purled braid."

She sure knew her history of ladies doodads.

"And look at that." Juliet nodded at the display case, where several colored bottles and a powder puff sat among other personal items once used by the notorious lady. "See the tortoise shell comb with a gold floral design and studded with rhinestones? Isn't that pretty?"

"I guess so, but I think those black garters are more interesting." Mark nodded toward the mannequin, who held up the hem of her red skirt, revealing red and black petticoats and a black silk garter with a gilt buckle and roses made out of ribbons. "The Shady Lady must have been one sexy woman."

Juliet swatted at him, grazing his arm and making him yearn for more of her touch. When she laughed, the lilt of her voice settled over him like fingers on an angel's harp. "You would find her undergarments intriguing."

"You're right about that. I don't know why she didn't wear those garters in the portrait that's hanging over the bar at The Hitching Post."

Juliet smiled impishly. "She probably knew the men would find her more appealing with that bedroom smile and only that gauzy thing draped over her."

Mark slid her a crooked grin. "Not me. I'm a black garter man."

Juliet arched a brow, brown eyes glimmering.

Was she making note of that tidbit of information?

He hoped so, then admonished himself for allowing his thoughts to drift in a sexual direction. For cripes sake, she'd just had a baby. And even if she hadn't, they were just friends.

"You know," Juliet said, "Lily Divine was an enterprising woman in her day. And I find her fascinating."

"Me, too," Mark said. Because she ran a whorehouse and a saloon, profiting from a man's lust. "But why do you find her so interesting?"

"Mr. Saunders told me that she was considered a troublemaker in her day. But I think that's probably because she was involved in the fight for women's suffrage."

"Well, that makes sense. I'm sure she had an interest in women's rights, especially since she was a businesswoman. After all, she owned the hotel, as well as the saloon. And then there was that private business she ran upstairs."

"Lily was only suspected of being a madam, since the previous owner of the saloon had run a brothel," Juliet argued. "No one really knows for sure. But I have a feeling that, more than anything, her forward-thinking caused folks to look down on her."

Before they could continue the conversation, Ben returned. "I'm sorry for the interruption. That call was from Matilda Matheson, an elderly lady who has a trunk full of memorabilia in her attic. She would like to make a donation, if we're interested."

"Is she bringing it in today?" Juliet asked.

"Oh, no. Tildy has arthritis and doesn't venture far from her house. And even if that weren't the case, she can't donate anything until her niece takes time to climb into the attic and go through the trunk."

"What's in it?" Juliet asked, obviously interested.

"Tildy can't remember," Ben said, with a chuckle. "Bless her heart."

Eager to get back to the discussion of the gold mine, Mark asked, "So who do you think is the legal owner of the Queen of Hearts?"

"Most of the rumors don't amount to much. And even if Crazy Red ran off with the deed, the old archives ought to prove that the title wasn't ever transferred properly. So I have to believe the mine was handed down to Caleb. And from what I understand, he's hired a lawyer to defend his claim."

Caleb certainly had the money to put up a legal fight for the land.

"Of course," Ben added, "Some of the old-timers would like to see Caleb Douglas get his comeuppance. But as far as the Thunder Canyon Historical Society and the museum go, we appreciate his generosity in helping us preserve our early history."

Mark and Juliet completed the tour, but instead of finding answers, Mark was left with more questions.

But one thing was true. Roy Canfield, the editor of the *Nugget* had been right. The real story revolved around the deed of the old gold mine.

And Mark planned to find out who really owned the Queen of Hearts.

* * *

"Do you mind if we stop at Super Save Mart on the way home?" Juliet asked.

"No. Not at all." Mark pulled out of the museum parking lot onto Elk, then turned south on Pine.

Juliet planned her speech carefully, trying to maneuver the conversation in the direction she wanted it to go. "Your parents sound like nice people."

"I suppose so." His eyes remained focused on the road.

"Maybe we should pay them a visit. Marissa and I could go with you. I think it would be a nice outing."

"Not today."

She slid a glance at him, saw that same hardened expression he'd worn when Gladys discussed his parents. But Juliet wasn't afraid to stand up to him. To push when necessary. "Maybe another day, then."

He didn't answer, and she realized he wouldn't commit. And that he had no intention of discussing his family situation with her.

Juliet was trying to be sensitive to his feelings. She really was. But his stubborn side was frustrating her to no end.

"I've never bowled," she said. "But it sounds like a lot of fun, especially in a league called the Gutter Busters. Maybe we could go watch some Wednesday. Or even play a game or two."

"I used to bowl once in a while," Mark said. "But I play golf now, whenever I get a chance. And the pro who gave me some pointers said the bowling was affecting my swing."

She wasn't sure if she wanted to prod him further or throw something at him. But she let it go.

For now.

Moments later, they parked in front of the grocery store. This time, Mark carried the baby, while Juliet filled the cart with things she needed to prepare a special dinner. She didn't know about Mark, but she was getting sick and tired of The Hitching Post meals. And even if she weren't, she didn't like him paying for everything.

She hadn't made a list, so they wandered from aisle to aisle, picking up pinto beans, rice and tortillas.

In the produce section, she selected tomatoes, green chilies, cilantro and onion. And in dairy, she grabbed a half gallon of milk, sour cream and a bag of Monterey Jack cheese.

As they neared the butcher case, a woman wearing an oversize black sweatshirt with a sunflower appliqué gasped and placed a hand on her chest.

Was something wrong?

The woman's gaze had locked on Mark's, and subsequently, so did Juliet's.

"Hello, Mom."

"Hi, Mark."

Juliet froze, a package of chicken breasts gripped in her hand. She studied mother and son, saw their tension-filled stances, felt the awkwardness. And it broke her heart. The reunion should have been exciting, something worthy of a hug, a bright-eyed smile.

"I...uh...was hoping you'd come by the motel," Mrs. Anderson said. "We've missed you. We both have."

"I've been busy."

The woman's eyes dropped to the bundle of pink flannel Mark held. Then she glanced at Juliet, a hundred questions in her gaze.

"This is my friend," Mark said. "Juliet Rivera."

"How do you do?" The woman reached out a hand. Her eyes begged for answers, for more of an explanation, for something Mark wasn't providing her. But she remained silent. Watery eyes told Juliet she was hurting, but not because Mark's presence had disturbed her.

"This is Juliet's baby," Mark said. But he didn't unwrap Marissa. Didn't reveal her sweet face.

Juliet stepped forward and withdrew the edge of the pink flannel blanket. "Her name is Marissa. And she's a week old today."

Mark's mother smiled, sentiment glistening in her eyes. "What a precious baby."

"She certainly is. Thank you." Juliet should have been pleased that Mark had introduced them, but she suspected he'd merely meant to avoid any of the questions that hung in the air.

How have you been?

Why haven't you called?

When will we see you again?

"I was just picking up things to make a special dinner to celebrate Marissa's birth," Juliet said. "Do you like Mexican food, Mrs. Anderson?"

"Yes, I do." The woman's green eyes grew wide and bounced from Mark to Juliet and back again. "My husband and I don't get a chance to eat it very often, especially when it's homemade. Having been brought up in Texas, we miss a good Mexican-style meal."

"Then maybe you'd like to join us for dinner," Juliet said.

Mark tensed.

"Why…" The woman paused, then looked at Mark as though wanting him to second the invitation.

He held his tongue.

Juliet wanted to kick him in the shins. Couldn't he see the woman was hurting? Maybe more than he was?

"My husband isn't feeling well," Mrs. Anderson said. "Perhaps another time."

"Of course." Juliet offered her a sincere smile, which was far more than her son had offered.

As Mrs. Anderson turned to leave, Juliet stopped her. "Wait, please." She reached into her purse, pulled out a slip of paper and a pen, then jotted down her telephone number. "Let me know when your husband is feeling better."

The woman took the paper, holding it close. In that moment, Juliet knew they'd all been hurt. Deeply. And by something she didn't understand. Something that needed to be fixed.

"Well, I'd better get back to the motel," Mark's mother told him. "Your father is working the front desk by himself, and it's been very busy today."

Mark nodded. "I'll stop by and see you before I leave town."

"Please do." Mrs. Anderson's lip trembled, then she looked at Juliet. "It was nice meeting you. And I *will* give you a call."

Juliet flashed her a sincere smile.

Then the woman pushed her empty cart away.

Mark's jaw locked, like the Tin Man's after a heavy rain.

But Juliet had a feeling he might not be silent when they got back to the car.

Chapter Ten

Mark gripped the steering wheel and stared straight ahead. He didn't want to fight with Juliet, but he didn't want her getting chummy with his folks, either.

Not while he was still in town.

He wasn't up for a family reunion. Not yet. And maybe not ever.

"I didn't mean to put you on the spot," Juliet said. "Are you angry with me?"

"No, not really." He was just frustrated, especially since he refused to share enough of his past to make her understand.

Years ago, Susan had tried to push him to reconcile with his family before their wedding, since Mark had refused to invite his parents.

"I don't want to chance ruining a day that's supposed to be happy," he'd told her.

Like Juliet, his fiancée hadn't understood the falling-out and had thought the absence of the groom's family would look weird to people. When Mark had finally leveled with her, opening his guts and explaining why he and his parents didn't have a close relationship, she'd backed down.

It might have been his imagination, but she'd never seemed to look at him the same after that. So, from then on, he'd intensified his resolve to keep his shameful secret to himself.

Still, Mark didn't want something from the past to affect his relationship—or rather his friendship—with Juliet. "It's your apartment, and you can socialize with anyone you want. But I don't appreciate you inviting my parents to dinner without talking to me first. That's all."

She nodded, as though she actually understood his feelings rather than the filtered half-truth.

"I'm sorry it bothered you." Juliet turned in her seat, facing him. "I should have waited to say something. But your mother seems very nice. And since I'm a new resident of Thunder Canyon, I like meeting people who live in the community."

He could understand that, but he still didn't like being pushed. Forced to do something that chapped his hide. "Why don't you invite my parents to dinner after I'm gone?"

She didn't respond right away, which made him think the conversation had died a slow death. Thank

God. But as they neared The Hitching Post, she brought it up again. "I wish you weren't so stubborn."

He bit back a hard-ass retort. It wasn't Juliet's fault that he didn't want to be around his parents. Well, his father, anyway. And she had no inkling of the kind of cruel accusations that had been slung at Mark years ago, accusations that still hurt, that still echoed in his mind.

You no good rebellious bastard.

You son of a bitch.

You let your sister die.

You killed her.

Get the hell out of my house. And don't ever come back.

To this day, he could still feel the grief, the guilt, the pain of rejection.

There probably weren't too many sixteen-year-olds who, after an outburst like that, would've dropped their heads and plodded to their rooms with their tails between their legs.

Mark certainly hadn't.

He'd thrown a few belongings into a knapsack, grabbed his jacket and stomped off into the stormy night, determined to either escape the godawful guilt or die in the process.

But he hadn't done either.

Around midnight, the sheriff found him thumbing a ride out of Thunder Canyon, sopping-wet and chilled to the bone.

"I can't believe you'd run off at a time when your family needs you," the uniformed officer had said.

Mark clamped down his shivering teeth, refusing to say anything in his own defense. And after a speech about minors and curfews, the sheriff had taken him back home.

It didn't take an honor student or an Eagle Scout to figure out his dad wasn't particularly pleased to see him walk in the front door, even though he hadn't said a damn thing. The hateful scowl his old man had worn was an image Mark would never forget.

"Sorry to hear about the loss of your daughter," the sheriff had told his parents. "It's a damn shame."

Jess Anderson had merely grunted, then climbed into the old family station wagon and driven down the mountain to the motel, where he'd holed up until the funeral.

His mother had burst into tears again, leaving Mark to face the sheriff alone. He'd actually wished the police officer would have pressed charges against him. Manslaughter. Negligent homicide. Something.

But he hadn't.

Still, every time his old man looked at him, each time his mother went into his sister's empty room and cried, whenever someone in the community whispered behind Mark's back, a gavel in his head pounded out his guilt.

And he couldn't blame them. It had been a tragic, rebellious mistake that couldn't be corrected.

Mark slid a glance at Juliet, and a jab of remorse struck him in the chest. She didn't know the demons he wrestled with, and he damn sure wasn't about to reveal them to her. But she didn't deserve the harsh words he'd lashed out at her. "I'm sorry, but my dad made it clear years ago that I was a disappointment to him. That he wanted me out of his house and his life for good."

"Maybe time has changed things."

"Not my memory."

"What about your sister's memory?"

His heart pounded in his chest, and his hands grew clammy as they gripped the steering wheel. "What about it?"

"Did your sister find it hard to forgive and forget, too?"

Juliet had no idea how badly the past haunted him. But he wouldn't let on. He couldn't. "No, my sister always got along fine with my parents. They favored her."

And he could now understand why. Prior to her wedding, she'd always done whatever they asked, whatever was necessary to keep the home fires burning while they worked at the motel from dawn to dark.

On the other hand, Mark had resented being stuck on the mountain, so far away from town, especially when his dad could have made life easier by living within city limits.

"I'm sure your parents miss her," Juliet said.

No doubt about that. His mom had been looking forward to being a grandma, even if Kelly wasn't too keen on being a mother. But Mark didn't want to go there, didn't want to encourage Juliet's curiosity.

"And since you're all they have left," she continued, "I'm sure they'd welcome a reconciliation."

"For cripes sake, Juliet. You don't know them. You don't know me. You don't know anything about what tore our family apart."

"You're right," she said. "But I'm just trying to help. Sometimes getting things out in the open gives a person a new perspective."

He felt badly about snapping at her, but wouldn't apologize. Why encourage her to push harder, to probe deeper? So he held his tongue, hoping to assuage the guilt. Hoping to end the conversation. But Juliet's eyes drilled into him, lancing the wound and releasing a brand-new assault of pain, guilt. Regret.

"What did they do to hurt you like this?" she asked. "To make you hold a twenty-year grudge?"

"They didn't do squat."

"Then did you do something?"

The truth of her question pierced him to the bone, but he refused to answer. "I'd rather not talk about it."

"Why not?"

"Dammit, Juliet. Would you get off my case?"

The words had no more than left his mouth, when he cringed at the sharp edge, at the bark, at the way he'd hurled them at her.

God, she wasn't going to fall apart on him and start sniffling, was she? He hoped not. He didn't deal well with tears—especially when he couldn't tell if they were real or fake. Susan, his ex, had been able to shed tears on demand.

When he snuck a glance across the seat, Juliet's gaze slammed into his.

Sharpened flecks of topaz blazed in her eyes, as she

pointed a finger at him and raised her voice. "Don't talk to me like that. I only meant to help. Not stir the guilt you feel."

So much for expecting her to fall apart.

He stole a glance in the rearview mirror, wondering how she'd come to that conclusion. Had she read the shame in his expression or his mind?

"If they didn't do squat," she pressed, "then I'm led to believe you're the one who's responsible for the rift."

"Yeah. In a way, I am."

"Your mother is hurting," Juliet said. "And you're hurting, too. Only you're covering it with anger and an I-don't-give-a-damn attitude."

She was probably right about his mom. And about him, too. But he wasn't going to discuss what happened that night, nor was he going to relive it.

On his eighteenth birthday, he'd finally left that mountaintop prison Jess and Anne-Marie Anderson called home, hitched a ride to the bus depot and took the old gray dog to Bozeman.

Before this damned assignment, he'd never looked back. And resurrecting old memories and pain wasn't something he intended to do now. Leaving home, leaving Thunder Canyon, had kept him from drowning in guilt. From reliving that fateful afternoon when a selfish decision on his part had led to his sister's death.

He slid another glance at the young woman across the seat, saw her furrowed brow, the pretty lips turned into a frown.

She had to know he was looking at her, but she didn't respond.

Well, so what?

He didn't need her sympathy.

Or her unspoken verdict.

When they arrived at her apartment, she maintained her silence, striking another blow to their friendship—or whatever the hell it was.

And right now, a bus ticket to Bozeman looked pretty damn appealing.

As soon as Mark had escorted Juliet and the baby inside the apartment, he left.

He hadn't said where he was going, and she hadn't asked. Nor had she mentioned her frustration, which was out of character for her.

Juliet had never been one to mince words when it came to expressing herself or her emotions. Feelings existed, and she didn't make a secret of hers.

Like her *abuelita,* she was quick with a hug when she felt love and affection. And she had no problem voicing an objection when crossed or slighted.

But this was different. She found it difficult to understand what had caused the ache in her chest or the tears that welled in her eyes. And she couldn't explain the guilt she felt over losing something she'd never really had.

This cold war she and Mark had silently declared made her uneasy and sad. And that didn't make much sense.

After all, Mark planned to leave Thunder Canyon as

soon as his story was finished. Only the town fool, *la tonta del barrio,* would expect their relationship to continue. Besides, she'd only known him for a couple of weeks. The secretive man was still a stranger in many ways.

So why did it bother her to think she'd lost his friendship?

Surely it wasn't because she'd fallen in love with him. She knew better than to let herself do something that crazy.

She just didn't like seeing him hurt, that's all. He'd proven to be a good friend—her only friend right now. And she'd only meant to help him in return. That's why she'd tried to get him to reconcile with his family.

Okay, so he'd been right. It wasn't her business. And her efforts had backfired. She knew better than to push him any more than she had.

But she cared for Mark, more than she dared admit—even to herself.

A *lot* more.

Oh, *Dios mio*.

Was it possible? Was she falling in love with the tortured, cynical reporter who had stepped in when she needed a friend the most?

It sure felt that way.

Great. Just what she needed. Another absent loved one.

Juliet put away her groceries—all but the items she needed for dinner—then soaked the pinto beans in a pot of water. Before she could do anything more,

Marissa began to cry, announcing it was chow-time again and causing Juliet to prioritize.

Her baby needed her, and their mother-daughter relationship was the only one that mattered.

For the past twenty-five years, Juliet had gotten along fine without Mark Anderson in her life. She could certainly survive the loss of his friendship, even if that meant never seeing him again, never seeing that teasing, flirtatious glimmer in his eyes, the way his lips quirked in a rebellious grin. Never hearing his graveled voice, his baritone laugh.

Grief and regret tore deep in her heart.

But she wouldn't let it mar her future or that of her daughter.

After feeding Marissa and getting an extraloud burp, Juliet laid the baby in the cradle she'd purchased at Second Chances, the thrift store down the street, and covered her with the light green *covijita*.

She marveled at the precious miracle that grew bigger each day and whispered a prayer of thanksgiving. Then she caressed her daughter's head, felt the downy fine hair. *Duerme bien, mi angelita*.

After leaving the bedroom and entering the kitchen, she put the beans on to cook, and lost herself in the sounds and aromas of a meal meant to be therapeutic. All the while she hummed a medley of mariachi tunes that *Abuelita* used to sing.

She prepared several chicken breasts, soaking them in a sauce of tomatoes and chilies, taking care to make the salsa especially mild. The lactation expert at the hospital said that if a food made Juliet gassy, it would probably do the same to the baby. Of course, the spices in this dish had never bothered her.

While the *pollo* marinated, she chopped additional chilies and tomatoes, along with onions and cilantro. It seemed like an awful lot of trouble to go to for a meal she'd most likely eat alone, but it didn't matter. She felt at home in the kitchen, and the scent of beans and fresh salsa reminded her of her grandmother. Of love and laughter on Sunday afternoons at home in the barrio.

Juliet might be the only one seated at the table, but she would prepare a meal that would make *Abuelita* proud. A meal that would heal her frazzled emotions and fortify her heart. After all, she was creating a new home in Thunder Canyon, one based on love, family values and a hint of Old World culture.

And she darn sure didn't need a stubborn, globe-trotting reporter to turn her life upside down.

Even if he already had.

An hour later, Mark stretched out on the king-size bed in his room at the Wander-On Inn. Using the remote control, he turned on the television set and surfed the channels, looking for something to take his mind off his work and the argument he'd had with Juliet. But he'd be damned if there was anything on that even came close to handing him an easy escape.

Watching the evening news made him long for another assignment, one that would allow him to make a difference in people's lives. One that would enable him to ride off in the sunset and leave Thunder Canyon in the dust.

A *Gunsmoke* rerun triggered thoughts of Old Town and of Juliet's love of the Wild West.

Bowling For Dollars reminded him of her silly urge to visit Buckhorn Lanes and watch the Gutter Busters do their thing. Or—God forbid—join the league his parents belonged to.

Trading Spaces merely made him think about how badly Juliet's apartment needed a remodel.

Dammit. He turned off the TV and stood. There wasn't anything worth watching, anything that didn't remind him of Juliet in one way or another.

He didn't like fighting with her. Didn't like stomping off and leaving things unresolved—a defense mechanism that had always worked well for him in the past.

And he damn sure didn't like thinking that their relationship—or whatever the hell it was—had been irrevocably damaged.

He probably ought to go to her place and tell her he was sorry. Not about being stubborn and refusing to socialize with his parents, but about snapping at her.

She'd only meant to be helpful.

But apologies didn't come easy for Mark.

He strode into the small bathroom and turned on the spigot, setting the shower in motion. Then he stripped off his clothes and climbed under the steaming spray.

The steady pulse of water helped some, but not enough. As he toweled himself dry, his thoughts remained on the argument they'd had, on the way Juliet's eyes had flashed in anger. And on the pain he'd spotted in her gaze when he'd taken her home. That last, sorrow-filled glance that had nearly torn him apart.

He blew out a ragged sigh. Damn. He didn't want her angry. Or her feelings to be hurt.

Against his principles, he threw on a pair of jeans and a shirt, then brushed his teeth and ran a comb through his hair. He didn't see any need to shave.

Five minutes later, he stood at Juliet's door, feeling like a kid who'd hit a baseball through his neighbor's window, asking for the ball and promising to replace the glass with a hard-earned allowance.

He knocked, and several moments later, she answered, wearing a pair of black slacks and a pink blouse, its buttons pulled taut by her breasts.

A shy but pretty smile made him momentarily forget why he'd come, so he just stood there. Their gazes locked. Caught up in something he couldn't explain.

The scent of peach blossoms and spice taunted his senses, making him take a second whiff.

And a third.

She ran her tongue across her bottom lip, and sexual awareness slammed into his chest, taking his breath away, along with the words he'd intended to speak.

She swung open the door, allowing him inside.

A part of him wanted to rewind, to start over. To head back to the Wander-On Inn and pretend he hadn't come to talk to her.

But he had. And he realized how much he'd missed their easy banter, their camaraderie. How much he'd missed *her*.

"I...uh...came to..." Oh, for cripes sake. Why couldn't he just spit it out? Why this awkward, adolescent reaction to the sight of her?

Her hair was loose and hung like a veil of silk past her shoulders, the glossy strands begging to be touched.

She didn't speak and merely stared at him in the same way he looked at her. Why wasn't she making this easier on him?

"I'm sorry," he finally said, his voice coming out soft and hoarse at the same time. "I didn't mean to be so hard on you."

"I'm sorry, too. My brother used to get mad at me when I didn't mind my own business. It's tough to keep quiet, though, when I care about someone and want to help."

He raked a hand through his hair, realizing now wasn't the time to tell her he didn't need anyone's help. He was ready to put this argument behind them. For good.

"Go ahead and invite my folks to dinner," he said. "That is, if you want to."

"And you'll come, too?" Hope glistened in a bright-eyed smile that dimpled her cheeks.

"Yes," he said. "I'll come, too, just as long as it's on my last night in town."

She didn't respond to the stipulation he considered a hell of a compromise. Still, he stepped over the threshold and closed the door behind him.

Once inside, the warm, fresh aroma of chilies and spice waylaid him, and his stomach growled in response.

Had she expected him? Had she made enough for two? Would she ask him to stay?

His stomach growled again, this time too loud for her to have missed.

"Dinner will be ready in a minute or two. Will you join me?"

Maybe she was just trying to be polite, but right now, he didn't care. The meal smelled incredibly good, and he was too hungry to be sensitive. "Yeah, I *would* like to eat with you. Thanks."

He watched in silence as she set the table. Then, taking a seat across from her, he relished one of the best chicken dishes he'd ever had. The sauce was on the mild side, but it was tasty just the same.

Throughout dinner, they seemed to tap dance around the sticky subject of his parents and the rift they'd had, which was a big relief. Mark preferred to glance up from his plate and see her smile, rather than frown.

After they ate, she stood and began to clear the table.

He reached for her arm and stopped her. "Let me help."

"All right."

They carried plates, silverware and glasses to the kitchen, and when they got to the sink, they reached for the faucet at the same time, fingers brushing, gazes locking, hearts pounding. Awareness flaring.

Time seemed to stand still, and a megadose of adrenaline blasted his libido, sending it into overdrive.

Mark didn't know why he did it. Didn't know why he couldn't keep his hands to himself. But he wanted to kiss her in the worst way.

And in the best way.

He cupped her jaw, his thumbs caressing the silky skin of her cheeks. Her lips parted, but she didn't speak. Didn't step away.

So he drew her mouth to his.

Chapter Eleven

Juliet knew better than to kiss Mark again, but her knees turned to mush when he cupped her jaw with gentle hands and placed his lips on hers.

And even though she knew it was foolish to encourage a relationship destined to end before it started, she couldn't fight the attraction or the desire.

The light bristle of his beard scratched against her skin in a pleasurable way. And she threaded her fingers through his hair, still damp from the shower, and drew his face closer still.

His hands stroked her back, her hips, and his tongue swept the inside of her mouth.

The musky scent of his mountain-crisp cologne drove her wild. She couldn't seem to get enough of him, of his taste, of his caress.

A whimper escaped from somewhere deep in her heart, which only seemed to enflame him, to urge him on. And his growing desire only heightened hers.

Their tongues mated in a desperate hunger, giving and taking. And when he moaned and drew her hips flush against him, she reveled in her power to excite him, pressing into his erection, wanting him. Wanting this.

An ache grew low in her belly, reminding her how long it had been since she'd had sex. And how recently she'd delivered her daughter.

Making love was out of the question, at least for another week or so. But that didn't mean she couldn't enjoy the taste of him and the overwhelming passion that blazed between them.

As he intensified the kiss and the gentle assault on her senses, she realized something special had happened. Something powerful.

If there were ever any question whether she'd fallen in love with Mark before, she knew the answer now. She loved his rebel grin, his wounded heart, his awkward but sweet efforts to look out for her and the baby.

And she certainly loved the effect he had on her body.

God help her, she was falling—heart first and eyes closed—for a man who would soon leave town, who would ride off into the sunset without her.

She ought to push him away, to put a stop to the passion that continued to build, but she wanted Mark and whatever he had to offer. And she meant to make the most of a kiss that rivaled anything she'd ever known.

No, she wouldn't put an end to the heated embrace until he did. And she certainly didn't sense any reluctance on his part.

Mark didn't know what had caught hold of him, but he didn't want it to end. Not the kiss, not the fire that raged in his blood.

Passion flared between them, promising a breathtaking sexual experience that would take them to places few people had reached. And that's just where he wanted this heated exploration to progress—to bed, where he could make love with her all night long, where he could bury himself in her softness and hear her cry out in a fulfilling climax.

The baby cried out from the bedroom, reminding Mark that they weren't alone, that things were far more complex than he'd let himself believe.

He couldn't allow their desire to run its course, so he pulled back, wanting to do the right thing, yet filled with regret. "I…uh…guess we shouldn't be kissing like that."

"I suppose not." A flush on her neck validated his suspicion—that she'd been just as carried away as he'd been.

He tried to clear the awkwardness from his throat. "Aren't you still…healing and stuff?"

"I feel back to normal, but Dr. Hart suggested I wait three weeks for…you know, sex. But I told her I'd be waiting a whole lot longer, since I haven't been… hadn't been…seeing anyone like that."

Until now.

Mark ran a hand along his jaw, felt the bristles he should have shaved, had he known they were going to kiss. A bucket of cold reality splashed over his head, and he wasn't sure what to say. He damned well couldn't start making promises about the future.

His game plan certainly hadn't changed.

And it wouldn't.

But that didn't mean they couldn't have a brief sexual relationship, assuming she was agreeable.

If she hadn't been told to wait another week for sex, would they have made love tonight? Would he have eventually realized he didn't have any condoms on him?

He might have one or two in his shaving kit, which was back at the inn, but a hike across the street would have diffused the moment.

He blew out a ragged sigh. This was a hell of a time to risk an unplanned pregnancy.

Talk about complex complications.

He cleared his throat, hoping it would clear his head. "I guess we've got another week to think about it then, don't we?"

"It seems that way." Her smile was a bit hard to read. Hopeful maybe?

Or was it remorseful?

Mark wasn't sure. But maybe in the next week or so, he ought to think of a way to casually bring his shaving kit back to Juliet's place.

Just in case he was invited to stay over for breakfast.

* * *

Several days later, Mark sat at the desk in his room at the inn, going over his notes. The scope of his story had changed in the past few weeks. And over the course of his stay in Thunder Canyon, he'd interviewed a slew of people, some more interesting than the rest.

Caleb Douglas had been the first he'd spoken to. At the time, the wealthy rancher and businessman seemed more interested in the grand opening of his ski resort, but that had changed with the influx of fortune hunters. Now, after talking to Caleb several more times, Mark had learned that the man was frustrated about the snafu with the land records down at the town hall.

And who could blame him?

Harvey Watson, the clerk who'd been transcribing all the old records into the new computer system, was on vacation, and rumor had it he might not be coming back anytime soon.

Mark slowly shook his head and clucked his tongue. In any other town, he would be able to access the records via the county computer system. But not in good old Thunder Canyon, which was still rooted in the early twentieth century when it came to modern technology and innovation.

So, early on, Mark had focused his research elsewhere, starting with respected members of the community, like Mayor Phylo T. Brookhurst.

He'd even interviewed some of the prospectors who'd come to town, looking to make their fortunes.

One of the wackiest interviews had been with Milcs "Mickey" Latimer, a crusty old miner who seemed to be losing it. But it wasn't just the fact that Mickey was tottering on senility that had made Mark come to that conclusion. Latimer had probably been goofy all of his life. For years, the old man had continued to mine for gold, never finding much of anything, but still working with a pickax and a mule and looking for a mother lode that probably didn't exist.

What made guys like that practically turn their backs on society? Hell, no wonder Latimer seemed so out of touch.

Mark flipped the pages of his notebook. He'd also interviewed knowledgeable men like Roy Canfield, the editor of the *Nugget.* And Ben Saunders, the high school teacher and museum docent who knew just about everything there was to know about the town's history.

But maybe he ought to focus his attention on some of the older folks in town and see if they could shed some light on the ownership of the Queen of Hearts.

Ben had mentioned Tildy Matheson, a woman in her eighties who'd lived in Thunder Canyon all of her life. She might have a better handle on some of those rumors and legends.

Mark picked up the phone, dialed 4-1-1 and asked for Miss Matheson's number. He jotted it down, then gave her a call and introduced himself. "I'd like to interview some of the citizens who've lived in town for a good number of years. I think it would help me get a better understanding of the history of Thunder

Canyon. Would it be all right if I came by and talked to you?"

"I'd be delighted," the elderly woman said. "I don't get many visitors."

"When would it be convenient for me to stop by?"

"If you'd like to come now, I'll put on a pot of tea."

Mark wasn't the tea and crumpets sort, but he hated to offend the elderly woman who didn't get many visitors. "I might bring someone with me, if that's all right with you. She's just had a baby and doesn't get out too much."

"That would be lovely," Miss Matheson said. "The babies in my family have all grown up. They sure don't stay little for long."

After setting an appointment for thirty minutes from now, Mark called Juliet and invited her to go along. He was glad when she agreed.

Twenty minutes later, they were on their way. Several times, Mark glanced across the seat, admiring his attractive companion.

Juliet looked especially pretty today, dressed in a pair of boots, a midlength black skirt and a cream-colored blouse. In fact, if she didn't have Marissa with her, most people probably wouldn't believe she'd just had a baby.

When she spotted him looking at her, she smiled, a rosy flush coloring her dimpled cheeks.

Mark found it hard to keep his mind on driving and hoped having the pretty mother and child come along on the interview wouldn't prove to be a distraction. They'd almost reached their destination, so he'd find out soon enough.

Miss Matheson's house was located on Chinaberry Lane in the old part of town.

Juliet pointed to the Victorian home bearing the address the woman had given Mark. "Is that two-story house hers?"

"I believe so."

"Just look at that architecture," Juliet said. "Isn't it charming?"

As far as Mark was concerned, the house might be interesting, but it needed paint and a handyman's touch.

The yard was a bit overgrown, with rosebushes that hadn't been pruned in at least a year and a lawn that needed mowing. It was a shame the elderly woman didn't have anyone to help her maintain the place.

Juliet peered out the window at the grounds. "I'll bet her yard was a floral wonderland at one time."

Her optimism was amazing, but she was right. In its day, the Matheson house had been a showcase.

After they parked, Juliet lifted the baby from the car seat, and Mark carried the diaper bag. They climbed the steps, and when they reached an old, ornate door that needed varnish, Mark knocked. But he beat Juliet to the punch. "Probably handcrafted. Nice workmanship, huh?"

"Beautiful," she said, studying the stained glass window that adorned the carved oak.

The door opened, and they were greeted by a gray-haired woman wearing bright pink slacks, a pastel-striped blouse and a white sweater.

"Hello, Miss Matheson. I'm Mark Anderson, and this is Juliet."

"How do you do?" She glanced only briefly at the adults on the stoop, her tired gaze immediately settling on Marissa. "Oh, what a beautiful baby. And she's a perfect blend of her mother and father."

Juliet glanced at Mark, as though allowing him to correct the woman, but for some dumb reason he held his tongue.

He told himself it wasn't necessary to complicate matters. Or was it more than that?

Did he, deep down, like the idea of being mistaken for Marissa's father? Or of being thought of as Juliet's husband?

Impossible. He wasn't a family man. Nor was he good husband material. His ex-wife could certainly attest to that.

"Please," Miss Matheson said. "Come in."

Mark waited for Juliet to step inside first, then followed her into the house that held a unique fragrance of timeless memories and lilac sachets. His grandmother's house back in El Paso had a similar lingering smell—one he found comforting.

Miss Matheson walked slowly, a cane in her gnarled hand to steady her steps, and led them into a living room, where a silver tray and china tea service sat on the coffee table. "Have a seat while I pour you some tea."

"Please," Juliet said, to the elderly woman, as she handed the baby to Mark. "Let me help."

"Why, thank you, dear."

Mark sat on the sofa, which was upholstered in a blue and green floral print that matched the drapes. He rested Marissa in the crook of his arm.

Miss Matheson placed her cane near the armrest of an easy chair, then carefully lowered herself into the seat.

"Thanks for seeing me," Mark said.

"I don't get out much," the older woman said. "So I'm always glad when someone stops in."

Juliet picked up the teapot that was adorned with a pink floral trim. "What a beautiful china pattern. Is this an antique?"

"Yes, it belonged to my grandmother. And it brings me a great deal of pleasure to use, even more so than having a perfectly steeped cup of tea." The old woman smiled wistfully. "But you probably won't understand that."

"Oh, but I do." Juliet returned her smile. "I lost my grandmother when I was ten and still have the quilt she made and several other personal items. They each remind me of her."

"Then hold on to those memories," the older woman said.

Juliet handed her a cup and saucer. "You have a lovely home, Miss Matheson."

"Thank you, dear. But let's not be so formal. My name is Matilda and everyone calls me Tildy."

Juliet smiled and nodded, but continued to peruse the room.

Next to a Tiffany floor lamp was a bookcase adorned with framed photographs, many of them yellowed by time. Mark suspected they were Tildy's family members, some of whom had probably passed on, yet remained as precious memories.

He wondered what Juliet was thinking and suspected the two women, one just beginning her life and the other facing the end, had a lot in common.

"I'm glad you came today," Tildy said. "I'm planning a trip to visit my sister in Billings, and I'm not sure how long I'll be gone."

Mark balanced the baby in the crook of one arm, while holding the delicate handle of the china cup in the fingers of his other hand. He studied the hot, amber liquid, but didn't take a sip. Instead, he addressed Tildy. "Do you know Caleb Douglas?"

"Of course. I've known the Douglas family for years. My grandmother used to be a friend of Catherine Douglas." The elderly woman smiled and added, "Amos and Catherine were the original Douglas settlers in Thunder Canyon."

Mark hoped he was finally getting somewhere. "Then I'm sure you're aware that the Queen of Hearts mine is supposed to belong to Caleb."

"Yes. It's been in the Douglas family for years."

"Did you know Caleb is having difficulty finding the deed?"

"No." Tildy took a sip of her tea. "I don't have much time to socialize anymore."

Mark wondered if this visit had been a waste of time. "Do you think it's possible that Amos may have forgotten to file the necessary paperwork?"

"That doesn't seem likely. From what I remember being told, Amos was a stickler for details."

If that was true, then where the hell was the deed? Could one of Amos's descendants have misplaced it?

He studied the woman who sipped her tea. Did she actually know anything about the mine or deed?

"Who do you believe owns the Queen of Hearts?" he asked her.

"Why, Caleb Douglas."

That certainly seemed to be the assumption of everyone in town.

Just then the telephone rang, and Tildy reached for the portable receiver resting on a small table to the left of her chair. "Excuse me, please."

"Certainly." Mark took a sip of sweetened tea and tried not to grimace at the taste. He preferred a hearty brew of coffee—black and loaded with caffeine.

"Hello?" the older woman said. "Oh, dear. Is today Tuesday?"

Mark wasn't sure what was being said on the other end of the line, but he figured Tildy had obviously forgotten something.

"What time will you be coming for me?"

So much for the interview.

"Twenty minutes? I'll have to hurry, but I'll be ready when you get here." She ended the call, then apologized. "That was my niece. I'm afraid I'll have to cut our visit short. I've got a doctor's appointment today."

"That's okay," Mark said. "I understand. But before I go, I want to ask you another question. Have you ever heard of Crazy Red Phelps?"

"The outlaw?" Tildy asked. "Sure, I've heard of

him. He was before my time, of course. But he once shot up the saloon. And if I remember correctly, he had some kind of feud with Amos, although I'm not sure what it was all about."

"According to Ben Saunders, Crazy Red once claimed that the Queen of Hearts belonged to him and that he meant to have it, one way or another."

Tildy took a sip of her tea. "I'm afraid my memory isn't what it used to be. But from what I was told, that outlaw was as crazy as they made them and twice as ornery. He might have imagined that he had a prior claim on the mine."

"That's possible. And maybe he stole the deed from Amos."

"I have no idea."

Mark sat back in his seat. Tildy Matheson hadn't offered him anything new or solid, but she'd sure set his mind spinning.

"Maybe we ought to let Tildy get dressed for her appointment," Juliet said, picking up the teacups and placing them on the tray. "I'll just carry these into the kitchen for you."

"Thank you, dear." The older woman slowly got to her feet and pointed a crippled finger toward the dining room table and beyond. "It's through that doorway."

Mark stood, too, and waited for Juliet to return from the kitchen. Researching Crazy Red Phelps would be his top priority.

And maybe, in the process, he'd learn who held the deed to the Queen of Hearts.

* * *

The next afternoon, Mark drove out to the Ranch View Estates on White Water Drive. He turned into the entrance on Stagecoach and followed the flags to the models at the end of the cul-de-sac.

A sales rep looking like a dime-store cowboy in a pair of shiny boots, a bolo tie and a black hat handed him a brochure, along with a map of the subdivision. "Just take your time. And if you have any questions, or if I can help, just let me know. My name is Bill Jarvis."

Mark nodded, then set out on the walkway to look over the professionally decorated houses.

Wouldn't Juliet be surprised if he handed her the keys to one of these new homes? A small one, of course, although they all looked fairly big, especially to a man who'd lived out of a suitcase and spent most of his nights in a hotel.

As he wandered through the first couple of models, he wasn't sure what he was looking for and wondered if he should have brought Juliet with him. But in the third home, the decorator had made one of the smaller bedrooms into a nursery.

The walls had been painted an airy, cotton-candy pink. A crib, made out of light wood, sported a fluffy comforter with pretty, pastel-colored butterflies. A matching frou-frou over the window was a nice touch. And so was the toy box full of stuffed animals and the baby doll perched on the dresser.

Yeah, Mark knew that decorator stuff wasn't included in the house he planned to buy. But that didn't mean this model wouldn't be a great home to raise a little girl in.

He strolled through the last two, but by the time he entered the sales office, his mind was practically made up.

Or should he include Juliet in the decision?

After all, she and the baby would be the ones living in the house.

The wannabe cowboy/sales rep was busy talking to a silver-haired lady who was visibly shaken.

She dabbed at her eyes with a tissue. "Bill, I don't understand why you can't let me out of the deal. I don't need the house now. My husband passed away last Friday, and my daughter wants me to move in with her in Colorado."

"Ma'am, I'd like to help you. I really would. But your escrow closed two weeks ago, and it's out of my hands. That house is your problem."

The woman, her eyes red and watery, sniffled. "I don't know anything about real estate, or escrows or mortgages. My husband and I were married for nearly fifty-two years, and he always handled those sorts of things for me."

When the lady wiped her tears again, the dime-store cowboy rolled his eyes and flashed a can-you-believe-this-old-lady? look at Mark before continuing. "I'm sorry to hear about your husband, Mrs. Grabowski. But I sell houses. I don't buy them back. Now, why don't you go home, skim the yellow pages and find yourself a good Realtor?"

Mrs. Grabowski sniffled again and lifted her chin,

then as Cowboy Bill opened the door and ushered her out in a manner that was just a tad more polite than booting her in the butt with those fancy boots, she turned to him.

Her tired blue eyes flashed a look of betrayal. "You were sure fussing over us when you wanted us to buy the house, saying things like, 'If there's anything I can do to help, anything at all, you just give me a whistle.'"

He lifted his palms in a slick, don't-get-me-dirty manner. "My hands are tied, Mrs. Grabowski."

She shook her head, then walked toward her car.

Mark couldn't help sympathizing with the grieving widow. He knew the sales rep couldn't very well buy back her house, but he didn't have to roll his eyes and make light of the poor woman's dilemma.

In fact, Mark wasn't sure he wanted to deal with a guy who couldn't be more sensitive, more respectful than that. So he sidestepped ol' Cowboy Bill and followed Mrs. Grabowski to the parking lot, watching as she climbed into a late-model Chevrolet.

She probably hadn't thought about things like probate, either. It could take a long while for her to sell the house. And Mark sympathized with her.

His grandma hadn't had much business sense, either. And when his grandpa had died, she didn't even know how to write a check or drive the car. That was one reason he'd resented moving from El Paso to Thunder Canyon and leaving his grandmother to fend for herself.

And that move to Montana, he realized, at that particular time, had been the turning point in his relationship with his dad. The moment when teenaged rebellion turned to resentment and disrespect.

Mark couldn't imagine how difficult it would be to survive the loss of a spouse and be slapped with financial decisions and problems all at once.

As he prepared to slide into the driver's seat of his rented sedan, he heard the woman's engine grind. Battery problems, he guessed. Car trouble was obviously something else she wasn't used to handling.

Mark couldn't very well leave her stranded like that. Cowboy Bill would probably tell her to call the automobile club, then make her hike to a payphone to do so.

The jerk.

So Mark climbed from the car and walked to her vehicle. "Sounds like you've got a bad battery."

"Oh, dear." The look on her face was enough to make a guy's conscience squirm.

"Do you have jumper cables?" he asked, knowing there weren't any in the sedan.

"I don't know. But my husband always kept tools and whatnot in the car."

"Let's look in the trunk."

With a little encouragement, she managed to flip open the lid. Sure enough, her husband had thought of everything—except ensuring his wife could get by without him. But Mark kept quiet about that.

Moments later, with her standing beside him and peering under the hood, he got the engine running. "You probably ought to drive straight to a service station and have someone check your battery."

"I will." She offered him a weepy-eyed smile. "Thank you, young man. I was just sitting there, praying that the engine would start. You've been a real blessing, an answer to a prayer."

Mark didn't know about that. He and God had never seen eye to eye, so he couldn't imagine The Man Upstairs using a hard-ass reporter to answer a grieving woman's request. But if she thought so, what the heck.

"My name is Iris Grabowski," she said.

"Mark Anderson." He reached out a hand to shake on it, and the woman offered him a hug instead, like he was some kind of hero.

"Bless you, young man. I'm going to be praying for you and your family."

Don't bother, he wanted to tell her. But he held his tongue. He sure as heck didn't need the poor widow to start crying again. "Thanks."

After she drove off, he climbed in the sedan and drove back to town. In the stillness of the car's interior, a pensive mood settled over him and he pondered all kinds of things—like widows and grandmas who'd been looked after all their lives and then thrust into a world they weren't prepared to handle. Of a stubborn son who shouldn't have moved his family thousands of miles away, leaving his widowed mother to fend for herself. Of an angry teen who resented leaving his grandmother all alone in the last years of her life.

Of the way a man's guilt and remorse seemed to ease when he helped someone less fortunate.

Then his thoughts took a philosophical turn.

If a guy did enough good deeds, could he eventually right his wrongs?

Not the unforgivable ones.

Chapter Twelve

After feeding Marissa, Juliet turned on the radio and found a classical station.

Music, she'd read, was good for babies. Maybe, with an early introduction, her daughter would grow to appreciate lyrics and rhythm and become a singer or musician someday.

Hey, it could happen. Papa had played the guitar, and Juliet, who'd sung in the high school choir one semester, had been invited to sing in the Troubadours, an elite high school group that performed in the community. She'd had to decline because of her job, but it had been an honor to be chosen.

She glanced at the small, plastic Tiny Tot mobile that rested on the dinette table. Mrs. Tasker had come by earlier today and brought the toy for Marissa. She'd told Juliet that her last grandson had used it when he was an infant, lying underneath it for hours and watching the colorful stuffed animals dangle overhead.

Juliet laid a quilt upon the living room floor, then after kissing Marissa's cheek, set the baby down and carefully placed the mobile-on-stilts over her.

Marissa blinked several times, noticing the movement of zoo animals that dangled over her head.

A knock sounded at the door, but before she could answer it, Mark let himself in.

"It's me," he said.

She could see that. A smile tugged at her lips as she admired his masculine form. He wore a pair of khaki slacks, a lightweight black sweater and a crooked grin that turned her inside out.

His hair was windblown, and he looked a bit tousled, in a most attractive sense. But then, everything about him seemed to appeal to her these days.

He held a maroon-and-green file of some kind at his side. As he opened his mouth to speak, his gaze landed on the baby. He cocked his head. "What's she doing on the floor?"

"She's playing. The child development book I checked out of the library said she'd stay awake a little bit more each week. So I thought it might be nice to offer her some stimulation. See how she tries to focus on the little animals?"

He nodded and studied the colorful zoo mobile. "Then I guess it's time we went shopping for some baby toys."

We?

Oh, cut it out, Juliet scolded herself. She shouldn't try to read into things Mark said.

"I imagine she'll need a lot more than toys," he added.

"You're right. And guess what." Juliet grinned, eager to share her good fortune, her acceptance in the community. "Mrs. Tasker came by to see us this morning. And she accidentally let it slip that on Saturday morning, before The Hitching Post opens, she's having what used to be a surprise baby shower for me. Isn't that sweet?"

"Yeah. That'll be nice." He looked up from the floor, where Marissa lay with her eyes closed, and flashed Juliet a smile. "Looks like Sweet Pea played so hard, she fell asleep."

"I suppose she's a little young for toys yet."

As Mark eased closer, she thought about giving him a hug in greeting, but kept her hands to herself.

Their relationship was at an awkward stage. She knew where she wanted it to go, but she had no idea how he felt, so it was probably best to let him take the lead.

For now, anyway.

He nodded toward the bookshelf, where the radio softly played a concerto. "Do you like this stuff? Or is the classical music for Marissa, too?"

"I want to introduce culture into her life early, and I don't think it's too soon."

He smiled, then lifted his free hand and ran his knuckles along her cheek, jump-starting her pulse and sending a rush of warmth through her veins. "You're going to make a great mom, Juliet."

Her heart soared. Did he think she'd make a good wife, too?

He dropped his hand, as though he'd done something out of line. He hadn't, though. And she wished she were bold enough to reach for his fingers, replace his touch and caress his face, too. But she decided it was best to wait until he gave her more encouragement.

So she asked, "Would you like something to eat or drink? I have iced tea and can make burritos with the leftover meat from last night."

"Not now. I ate while I was out."

All right. She'd try again. "How's your research going?"

"I'm plugging along. I talked to Ben Saunders earlier this morning, and he said various newspapers from the late eighteen hundreds were placed on microfiche and left in a box at the museum, although he couldn't remember where. He's going to call me when he finds it. The article he told me about, the one in which Crazy Red was quoted, is supposed to be in there somewhere."

Like a supportive wife who was interested in her husband's work, she asked, "What else is new?"

He flashed the file he'd been holding at his side, a brochure of some kind.

"What's that?"

He held the cover so she could see the words. *Ranch View Estates*.

"I'm thinking about buying a house in that new development." His words opened the floodgates, releasing a rush of hope in her heart.

Her unfulfilled dreams soared.

Had Mark changed his mind? Had he decided to stay in Thunder Canyon?

Apparently.

Did his plans to buy a house have anything to do with her? With them?

Oh, Dios mio. Could he be falling in love with her?

She wanted to say something, to babble her happiness, but she kept quiet, waiting. Waiting to hear the words she wanted him to say.

But his cell phone rang, interrupting their conversation. He flipped open the lid and spoke. "Anderson. Hey, Mary. What's up?"

Was Mary a co-worker?

The fact that she might not be echoed in Juliet's ears and thudded around in her chest.

"Sure. I've got a copy stored in my laptop, back at the inn. I can e-mail it as an attachment."

She blew out the breath she hadn't realized she'd been holding. The call was definitely work related.

"No problem." Mark disconnected the line, then placed the cell phone on the dinette table and opened the Ranch View Estates brochure.

"You were right about those houses," he said. "They're nice and the floor plans are roomy. And since I need a write-off, I think I'll buy one, which ought to make my accountant happy."

It would make Juliet happy, too. After all, it looked as though Mark had decided to make Thunder Canyon his base. And that meant, even if he had to travel on assignments, he would always come back home, and she'd get to see him again.

"Which model do you like?"

He wanted *her* opinion on the house? Was that because he wanted her to live with him? To marry him?

She had no idea, but even if he'd just contemplated the possibility that they might have a future together, it was a step in the right direction.

Trying not to let her optimism run amok, she said, "I like them all."

He pointed to a floor plan of the Sedona. "This one is a bit bigger than I wanted, but it ought to work."

Ought to work for what?

Before she could respond, his phone rang again.

"Hello." He frowned. "Right now? What's his rush?"

She bit her bottom lip, wishing they could get back to the discussion of the house.

"All right. But give me a few minutes to get back to my room." He disconnected the line and set the cell phone on the table. "Listen, Juliet, I need to send a file to my boss. Maybe we can go look at the houses together this weekend. Then, if I put a down payment on one, we can celebrate by having dinner at Sebastian's Steak House."

"Sure." She walked him to the door, afraid to dream, to believe. After all, he hadn't said anything about love. Or marriage. But he'd definitely decided to stay in Thunder Canyon—or at least establish residency here.

She couldn't wipe the silly grin from her face or the song from her heart.

Maybe she should be the one to mention love

first. After all, Mark might need a little encouragement—a gentle push that would have him admit falling in love with her, just as deeply as she had with him.

An hour later, while Juliet nursed Marissa, Mark's cell phone rang and rumbled on the dinette table, where it sat next to the Ranch View Estates brochure.

She wondered whether he'd realized he'd left it here. And if not, whether the call was important.

He hadn't invited her to his room across the street, and although she'd always wanted to see the inside of the hotel that had once been owned by The Shady Lady, she hadn't pressed for an invitation. When it came to men, Juliet had never been pushy.

But she had an excuse to visit now.

And if the opportunity arose, she would be honest about her feelings so he'd feel better about expressing his. And maybe, if things worked out the way she wanted them to, she could talk him into moving back to her apartment until the new house was ready.

Hope, which had always been something she'd latched on to, reared like a mystical, white stallion.

She went to the closet and pulled out the second-hand stroller. Then she carefully placed Marissa in the bed and used two rolled receiving blankets to support her comfortably. Then she knelt and placed a kiss on the baby's cheek.

"I'll wheel you into the bathroom, pumpkin. Mama's going to freshen up, then we're going bye-bye."

Twenty minutes later, Juliet pushed the stroller

around the side of the building, to the front of The Hitching Post and across the street.

The Wander-On Inn had been refurbished over the years, but it still maintained the charm of the other false-fronted buildings in Old Town. She'd heard it was more like a bed-and-breakfast than a hotel.

She entered the lobby, a small, cozy room with a couple of leather sofas, a fireplace and a decorator piece of carpet lying on top of hardwood floors. She made her way to the front desk, where a tall, lanky man with dark hair worked behind a computer screen.

When the clerk glanced up, Juliet said, "I'd like to see Mark Anderson. He's staying here."

"Just a moment, while I check to see if he's in."

"Thank you." She fiddled with the narrow strap of her shoulder bag. Maybe she should have called first. If Mark was out on another interview, she'd have to head back home.

"Mr. Anderson?" the man said into a house phone. "There's a lady with a baby here to see you."

"All right." The hotel clerk smiled at Juliet. "He's in suite 104, which is right through that doorway, the last room on the right. You won't have to take the stairs."

Juliet flashed him an appreciative grin. "Thank you." Then she wheeled the baby down the carpeted hall.

Before she had a chance to knock, Mark opened the door. He wore the same khaki slacks and black sweater that he'd had on before, but he'd kicked off his shoes. For a woman who'd been interested in looking over the hotel, she couldn't seem to keep her eyes off the man who stood before her.

"This is a pleasant surprise." His crooked grin warmed her inside and out, making her feel giddy and awkward at the same time.

A lock of his hair had tumbled onto his forehead, tempting Juliet to brush it aside.

Or did she just want an excuse to touch him?

She handed him the cell phone. "You left this at the apartment, and I wanted to return it to you, especially since you received at least one call that I know of."

"Thanks." He took the phone, then opened the door to let her and the sleeping baby into his room. "This is a first."

It was, she supposed. She'd never been bold enough to visit a man at work or at home. Erik had placed a lot of boundaries on their relationship, something that, in her naiveté, she hadn't questioned.

She scanned the small interior, realizing she'd entered a sitting room. "I didn't know the old hotel had suites."

"Originally, it didn't. But during the last remodel, the owner took two rooms and created this one. Depending upon the guest, they refer to it as either the bridal or presidential suite." He shrugged, eyes crinkling, a grin tugging his lips. "The company travel coordinator passed me off as a dignitary of some kind, so I got lucky. I can give you the grand tour, if you want to see it."

"Actually, I'd love to." She glanced at Marissa, saw her sleeping soundly and parked the stroller near the sofa. "From what I've been told, most of the hotel rooms have an old photograph or piece of furniture that has some history behind it."

"Maybe so," he said, "but I haven't found anything noteworthy in here."

She looked at the desk, where his laptop was connected to the Internet via the telephone. A take-out menu sat beside it, a brown smudge marring the print. The newspaper rested on the coffee table, next to a candy bar wrapper and a half-eaten bag of pistachios.

"I guess you could call this my office. Come on, I'll show you where I kick back and relax." He led her into the sleeping area.

Her eyes immediately lit on a blue-and-yellow spread that matched the drapes. It was a bit rumpled, and she could see the indentation his head had left on the pillow. He must have been kicking back before she knocked.

"Did I come at a bad time?" she asked.

"Not at all. I'm glad you're here."

So was she. Just being with him in his room, so close to the bed where he'd recently lain, was a bit heady. Exciting.

He tossed her a smile that tumbled around in her heart, stirring up all kinds of feelings—attraction and desire, to name two—and provoking a pressing urge to tell him she'd missed not having him sleeping at her place.

They stood there for a while, awareness growing. Hearts beating. That lazy shank of hair calling to her.

She reached up and bushed it aside, her fingers lingering a bit longer than necessary. Their eyes locked, and she couldn't move, couldn't speak. She was too caught up in whatever swirled around them—pheromones, desire. Sexual curiosity.

Surely, Mark felt it, too.

He reached out and stroked her hair, letting the strands sift through his fingers.

Her heart pounded in anticipation, waiting for him to make a move while contemplating making one of her own.

"It's been a week," he said, reminding her that the doctor had said sex was okay.

"I know."

"We were going to think about…some things."

"I haven't thought of much else," she admitted.

Was that making the first move?

His lips quirked into a crooked smile, then he bent to give her a kiss.

She lifted her arms, wrapping them around his neck, and leaned into his embrace. The kiss deepened, and she thought she'd die from want of him. From want of his love.

As tongues sparred and mated, she closed her eyes, oblivious to anyone or anything than this man who touched her in such a sensual way and held her heart in his hands.

Mark didn't want the kiss to end, didn't want to put a stop to the blood rushing in his veins. He relished the lady in his arms, each touch, each soft whimper.

No woman had ever moved him like this, provoking him to make love with a slow hand and a gentle touch, to prolong the pleasure for as long as he could hold out, making sure she enjoyed each moment in his arms, in his bed.

He wanted her. Badly. And with reluctance, he with drew his lips—but not his embrace—and rested his forehead against hers. "I want more than your kiss, Juliet."

"I want that, too."

His heart thumped into his throat, and he tilted her chin and kissed her again. His tongue swept the inside of her warm, willing mouth—seeking, exploring, savoring, demanding. He caressed the gentle slope of her back, the curves of her hips, then cupped her bottom and pulled her against his demanding erection.

Their first time together should be special, but all he could think of was losing himself in her, which both scared and excited him.

He nuzzled her neck, placing open-mouthed kisses along her jaw and throat. At the same time, he slid his hand under her yellow cotton top, felt the warmth of her skin, the silky softness. His fingers slid along her ribs, finding her bra and the fullness of her breasts. "Is it all right if I touch you here?"

"You can touch me anywhere you like," she said, her voice edged with the husky tone of passion.

He fumbled with the buttons of her blouse, then slid the fabric over her shoulders, removing it and revealing a white cotton bra. It wasn't one of those slinky, little ones made of flimsy lace and silky cups meant to arouse a man beyond measure, but seeing her breasts nearly bare and that sweet anticipation in her eyes, nearly knocked him to his knees.

She was offering him a gift, something a man like him didn't deserve but couldn't refuse. "You're beautiful, Juliet."

"You don't have to say that." Her hands slipped to the slight bulge of her tummy. It had gone down significantly over the past few weeks—not that he cared whether it had or hadn't.

"I'm five or ten pounds heavier than I used to be," she said. "And I've got stretch marks, too."

He knelt before her, caressed her belly and placed a kiss near her navel. Then he gazed up at her. "Childbirth and motherhood have only made you more womanly, more appealing."

Juliet closed her eyes, relishing the words Mark said, the sweet kiss he'd pressed on her tummy.

As his sensual praise chased away self-consciousness and doubt, she pulled his shirttail from his pants, trying her best to undo the buttons. She wanted him naked, wanted to feel him skin to skin, wanted to feel him inside of her.

Before long, they stood before each other, partially clothed and fully aroused. He kissed her cheek. "I've got a condom in my shaving kit."

She smiled. "Get it, while I turn down the covers of the bed."

She went to the sitting room and took a quick peek at her daughter, who continued to sleep soundly, unaware of the step her mother and the man who had helped bring her into the world would take, a step Juliet was eager to make.

When she returned to the bedroom, Mark stood by

the bed, the spread folded down, a foil packet in his hand. She smiled and made her way to the man she loved

Did he know how badly she wanted to give him her body, heart and soul?

Mark cupped Juliet's cheeks in his hands. Passion smoldered in her gaze, matching his own, he suspected. "I want this to be good for you."

"It's already been better than I'd ever imagined." Then she stepped out of her shoes and unzipped her pants.

He watched as she bared herself to him, and something stirred deep within him, something he had never experienced before. Something he didn't dare contemplate now.

She stood before him, naked, lovely, flushed with passion and desire, yet appearing to battle shyness.

"Are you sure about this?" he asked.

"Love me, Mark."

Her simple request was his undoing. He wanted to make love to her more than anything he'd ever wanted in his life.

Juliet watched as Mark undressed. He probably suspected she'd only been requesting sex. And she had been. But there was so much more to her words. She loved Mark deeply and wanted him to love her back.

He tore into the foil packet, protecting them, then took her mouth, his hunger not sated in the least, and drew her to the bed.

All right. So he hadn't said the words, hadn't pronounced his love. She'd be content with that.

For now.

If she only had this once, this afternoon, to make love with him, then she intended to give him all she had, and to take whatever he had to offer.

"I don't want to hurt you," he whispered. "So I'll try to be gentle."

She nodded, trusting him like she had no other.

He entered her, slowly at first. And it hurt briefly, but the urge to feel him inside of her was too great to care. She arched against him, drawing him deeper. The initial discomfort was surpassed by pleasure and fulfillment as he moved, giving, taking, driving her to the brink of some precipice she'd never before reached.

Her heart sang, as her body responded to each touch, each kiss, each thrust.

The loving rhythm built into a powerful rush, a crescendo that made them one, taking them to paradise and beyond. As they peaked together, a star-spinning climax burst across her vision, touching her heart and soul.

She'd read about orgasms and wondered why she'd never experienced one before, but now she knew. She'd never made love like this—not with a man she truly adored. So she held on to each wave of pleasure, wanting to keep him inside of her forever.

When their sweet joining was over, the loving didn't stop.

Unlike Marissa's father, Mark continued to hold her, murmuring how sweet she was, how beautiful.

An I-love-you could come later, she supposed. As

it was, she would bask in the afterglow of what they'd just shared and pretend that he'd said the words she longed to hear. That he'd committed to more than a one-time sexual fling.

As they lay in each other's arms, bodies glistening and the scent of their lovemaking lingering in the air, she was afraid to move, to speak. Afraid to break the magical spell that bound them together forever. Afraid to quell the sense of family and rightness that she'd been missing for what seemed like ages.

The ensuing silence grew heavy.

Over and again, words of love struggled to break free, but she bit them back for fear he wasn't ready to hear them yet. But that didn't mean she wasn't listening, waiting for him to share his thoughts about the future.

Mark, his passion spent and still reeling in the power of his release, felt the urge to say something, although he didn't know what. He was too afraid they'd have to discuss the turn their relationship had taken. And the fact that he'd be moving on to another assignment one day soon.

But he couldn't deny how good their lovemaking had been. How special. How unforgettable. And although he'd suspected she'd been just as caught up in the heat as he'd been, he needed to know for sure.

He rolled to the side, taking her with him, then ran a hand along the contour of her hip. "I hope that was something you'd walk across the room for."

She smiled. "I'd run a marathon for it."

"It'll be better next time." He brushed a strand of hair from her forehead. "I promise."

"Oh, yeah?" She brightened. "I'll have to hold you to it."

He liked the sound of that, the promise of another afternoon in Juliet's arms. And he hoped that she realized their sexual relationship, no matter how special, was just temporary. Mark didn't make commitments and promises he couldn't keep—although he had to admit, this was the first time he'd suffered even a pang of regret that he didn't.

"By the way," he said. "I didn't get a chance to tell you. But I'd like for you and Marissa to live in the house I'm going to buy."

"You would?" Her eyes glimmered, brighter still, and he could understand why. She'd probably give her right arm to move out of that rundown apartment over The Hitching Post.

"And you don't have to worry about rent," he added. "I'll need someone to look after the place, since I'll be gone most of the time."

Had the flicker in her eyes died down?

Maybe it was only the afternoon shadows that darkened the hotel room.

"So what do you say?" he asked.

Juliet pondered his question before responding. Something told her that she and Mark hadn't placed the same value on their relationship. It made her glad she'd held back the vows of love and forever she'd been tempted to utter during their lovemaking.

Well, glad and sad.

She finally managed to answer his question—sort of. "I'll have to think about it."

Hopefully, Mark was still tiptoeing through his feelings for her. Maybe he needed more time to consider something deeper, something stronger and more special.

But memories of her baby's father crept up on her. Erik Kramer had always sidestepped an I-love-you, and that fact didn't sit well with her.

Had she misjudged a man again? Given herself to someone who didn't want the same things in life that she did?

"I need the house as a tax write-off," Mark said, repeating something he'd already told her. "And since I won't be living in it, I'll need someone to take care of things for me."

She assumed he meant someone to take care of the house. But was he actually asking her to take care of his physical needs, too, while he lived another life that didn't include her?

Erik had wanted to set Juliet up in a condo. But he hadn't wanted to marry her, hadn't been free to do so.

Nor had he wanted to create a family with her.

She offered Mark a smile, but not a commitment of any kind. She needed some time to think. Some time to consider the ramifications of living in his house rent-free. Some time to see if his offer included stipulations she couldn't accept.

And, a Pollyanna voice reminded her, she needed time to see if there was a remote chance Mark might one day say the words she longed to hear.

Chapter Thirteen

Mark didn't move into Juliet's apartment, but his shaving kit sat on her bathroom countertop, and he'd spent the past two nights with her.

That had to count for something.

Sleeping in his arms was something Juliet could easily grow used to. In fact, it was something she hoped they'd both grow used to. And although she had some qualms about his lack of commitment, she decided to take one day at a time. She hoped that, given time, Mark would fall in love with her.

As she parked the Chevy S-10 pickup in the parking lot of the Lone Pine medical building, she glanced into the rearview mirror and checked her lipstick. Light and glossy. Hair was okay, too.

She took Marissa from the car seat and carried her inside.

Mark had offered to go with her to the appointment with the pediatrician, but she'd told him not to bother this time. He'd been researching the Internet and had just found an interesting site that listed the Rafferty Gang and brief bios of some of the outlaws, including Crazy Red Phelps.

As Juliet entered the central waiting room that several doctors used, she recognized a couple of regulars from The Hitching Post, most of whom thumbed through magazines, waiting their turns to be called.

But the attractive, salt-and-pepper-haired woman sitting near a potted palm stood out—Mark's mother.

Mrs. Anderson had recognized her, too.

Juliet smiled, mouthed a "hello" and waved at the woman. She wanted to be friendly, but was afraid to get too close. After all, challenging Mark about the falling out he'd had with his parents hadn't gone over well, and she was reluctant to do anything to put a strain on a developing romance.

Okay, so she was still hopeful that their relationship was moving toward happily ever after.

After signing in at the pediatric desk, Juliet searched for a chair. There was an empty seat beside Mrs. Anderson, but she chose one closer to the pediatrician's office. Surely, the woman wouldn't think that was odd or that Juliet was trying to avoid her.

Several minutes later, Mark's mother placed the magazine she'd been reading on a table, stood and made her way to Juliet. She nodded to an empty chair. "I hope you don't mind if I sit here."

Obviously, Mrs. Anderson didn't have anything to lose by striking up a conversation. And since Juliet had decided not to push Mark anymore about reconciling with his parents, what would it hurt?

"No, I don't mind at all." Juliet offered her a smile, then made sure Marissa's diaper bag was out of the way so the older woman wouldn't trip over it.

"Are you bringing the baby in for a checkup?" Mrs. Anderson continued to stand and study Marissa, a look of awe in her gaze.

"Yes. I'm curious to see how much she's grown, although I know she fits into her newborn gowns much better now."

"She's a beautiful baby."

"Thank you, Mrs. Anderson."

"It's Anne-Marie," she corrected, flashing Juliet a nervous smile. She took a seat and rested a black purse in her lap. "I'm not sure what my son has told you."

"Not much. Just that he's never gotten along with his father. And that you'd had a rift of some kind." Juliet didn't want to be disloyal to Mark, yet she was still curious as to what had caused the division.

"My husband and I would like to apologize for a lot of things, but Mark won't give us a chance." The older woman bit her bottom lip. "And I suppose, I can't blame him."

Juliet felt sorry for the mother who appeared to want to make things right with her son. And since

Mark was the only child the Andersons had left, Juliet could certainly understand that.

"I'm not sure how close the two of you are," Anne-Marie said, "but if you could talk to him, let him know that we love him, that we'd like to talk and try to put some of this behind us…."

"Mark is stubborn," Juliet said. "And I think he's been hurt deeply, although I don't know any of the details."

"It all started with the move," Mrs. Anderson said. "I should have leveled with the kids, but I was afraid to."

Juliet knew Mark didn't like Thunder Canyon and resented moving away from El Paso.

"Mark was always butting heads with my husband. And I was afraid that if he knew his father was having an affair with a young woman in town and that our marriage was on the rocks, he wouldn't take it well. That he would have rebelled. But now I think that may have been the wrong decision."

Juliet wasn't so sure about that. Did kids need to hear those kinds of details about the adults in their lives? Or should they be protected from things that really weren't their business?

"My husband's father had passed away, and his mother, although grieving and struggling to be on her own, came up with the idea. She begged Jess to give our marriage a chance, to leave town and the woman who'd come between us. A move was our only chance to remove the temptation and start fresh."

"And your husband agreed?"

"Reluctantly." Mrs. Anderson blew out a shaky sigh. "It was tough at first. Jess was so hard to live with. He'd made a sacrifice for the good of the family, but that didn't mean he was happy about it. And then we were struggling to make a go of the motel. The kids were miserable and missed their friends, their grandmother."

That still didn't seem like a good enough reason to stay angry, to maintain a grudge.

"But things are much better now," Anne-Marie said, a steady smile growing. "My husband and I have become involved in the community and in our church. I just wish Mark could get to know his father on an adult level."

So did Juliet. If anything, she was more convinced that the Andersons needed to have a heart-to-heart.

"My daughter's death is what finally tore our family apart," Anne-Marie added. "Mark felt responsible, and I'm afraid, in our anguish, we blamed him, too."

"Was it his fault?"

"No, it wasn't. But at the time, my husband and I were crazy with grief and frustration. We, or rather Jess, said some terrible things to Mark. And, obviously, those remarks are something my son can't forgive."

Juliet hurt for Mark, but she sympathized with his parents, too. Surely this was something that could be mended, patched up.

"I don't think there's a lot I can do to facilitate a reconciliation right now," she told the older woman, "but I truly believe Mark would be a happier man if he could make peace with his family. And when the time is right, I'll do my best to encourage him to talk to you and your husband."

"Bless you," Mrs. Anderson said. "Mark's wife tried to step in, right before their marriage, but Mark refused. And my husband and I weren't even invited to the wedding."

Mark's wife?

Juliet's heart pounded in her chest, but before she could comment or quiz the woman any further, a nurse called, "Anne-Marie Anderson."

"I have to go, but thank you so much for listening." Mark's mother patted Juliet's hand, then got up from her seat, leaving Juliet in the waiting room, feeling betrayed.

She'd been honest with Mark from the start. Why had he kept so many secrets from her?

And he had a wife? Was he married? Divorced? Separated?

He'd never said a word, never hinted.

Her pulse throbbed in her ears, as her anger built.

Were all men jerks?

Or just the ones she was attracted to?

Mark sat before the laptop computer, typing some notes into a file.

So far, he'd learned that Willard "Crazy Red" Phelps, the Confederate soldier turned outlaw, had been born near Thunder Canyon. His father had died "in the prime of life," and his mother had taken him and an older brother to live with her parents on a small farm outside of Atlanta. That's where he'd grown up.

Stretching and trying to work a kink out of his shoulders, Mark glanced at the clock in the kitchen. Juliet was due home soon, unless she stopped by Super Save Mart.

He heard a car drive up and peered out the dining room window. There she was. Just her and the baby. No groceries to help her carry in.

After saving his work, he shut down the computer, eager to hear what the doctor had said, and opened the door for Juliet.

She trudged up the steps, her movements tense, all signs of a smile absent.

"Is something wrong?" he asked.

"Yes."

Mark's heart damn near jumped from his chest. He could have sworn Marissa was gaining weight and growing longer. "What did the doctor say?"

"Nothing much." Juliet carried Marissa into the bedroom and laid her in the cradle.

"Then what's the matter?"

As she returned to the living room, her hands plopped on her hips and a fire raged in her eyes. "How *dare* you keep secrets from me."

"What the hell are you talking about?"

"I told you everything. About my family. About Marissa's father."

The woman might be petite and soft-spoken at times, but a Latin temper had surfaced, one he'd only caught a glimpse of in the past.

He didn't know who had talked to her, what she'd learned, but he wasn't going to run at the mouth until he had an idea where she was going with all of this.

"Why don't we start over," he said.

"Why don't *you* start over by telling me about your wife."

"I have no idea what's got you so riled up. Susan and I were divorced years ago."

Juliet's stance didn't waver. What the hell did she want to know? It's not as though he was still married. As though he was trying to pull a fast one, like Marissa's father had done.

Mark raked a hand through his hair. "Not long after landing a job with Golden Eagle News Service, I married a young woman I'd met in college."

Juliet listened, although her silent anger showed no sign of abating.

Mark blew out a sigh. "Susan was a homebody and a schoolteacher by degree. She wanted a home and a family and didn't appreciate my itinerant lifestyle."

"Why didn't you tell me?"

"The marriage didn't last a year, but that was long enough for me to realize I'm not husband material."

His words seemed to crush her. Or enrage her. It was hard to tell. Whatever she was feeling had her wrapped tighter than a top ready to launch.

She crossed her arms and shifted her weight to one leg. "You've kept secrets from me."

So what if he had? He kept secrets from everyone. It was the only way he could live with what he'd done.

Had her informant told her about Kelly, too? About the part he played in her death?

"Our friendship," Juliet added, "hasn't been a two-way street."

Their *friendship?*

Whatever they'd shared was more than that, although he didn't want to go there. Didn't want to consider what he was feeling for her and why her anger bothered him so much.

He wasn't sure what to say in his defense. His emotions were swirling around like a Texas twister.

"Why did you ask me to live in the house you want to buy?"

"To help you out," he said. "You and Marissa need a better place to live. And I hoped we could work out something beneficial for both of us. I hoped you'd look after my interests."

"You can take your interests and shove them where the sun doesn't shine." Her eyes sparked in ire, then she unleashed a flurry of words in Spanish, few of which he could decipher when she spoke that fast. She threw up her hands. *"Soy la tonta del barrio."*

The fool of the neighborhood?

Mark wasn't exactly sure what had set her off. Or who had told her he'd been married before, albeit briefly. But there was no talking to her, no reasoning with her like this. So he kept his mouth shut, listening and hoping a clue would surface.

"I think it's best if you take your things and go back to the inn."

Her words sucked the air out of the small apartment, but it was too late for her to reel them in, too late for him to apologize and start over.

And he wasn't sure he wanted to. Wasn't sure what would happen if he did.

The old fight-or-flight instinct had kicked in, and he was afraid to fight for something he didn't think would last. So he packed his laptop and his shaving kit, and left the small rundown apartment.

And as he did, no one felt more of a fool than he did.

Back at the inn, Mark paced the floor, his anger and frustration pouring out of every cell in his body.

Thank God he hadn't signed on the dotted line for one of those damned houses, or he'd be in the same fix as Iris Grabowski—stuck with a home he didn't need or want.

Stuck.

That's how he felt. Imprisoned in Thunder Canyon on a fool's errand.

But he wasn't going to stay any longer. He was out of here.

He snatched his cell phone and dialed his boss. After several rings, Tom Detwiler answered.

"It's Mark Anderson."

"Hey, thanks for getting that file to me so quickly. You're the best."

Yeah, well Mark sure hoped he felt that way after he asked to be reassigned, or else he'd quit the news service. He couldn't stay in Thunder Canyon one more minute.

"Listen, Tom. This story isn't panning out. There's nothing here, and I'm not going to waste my time or your money by staying here any longer."

"Are you sure about the story?"

"Damn sure." He just wasn't sure about anything else. About why his heart was ricocheting in his empty chest with hollow thumps. About why that ever-present sense of guilt seemed watered down with regret.

"Okay," Tom said. "But sit tight, will you? I have a feeling something *big* is coming down the pike. And it might be your lucky day."

If anyone needed a turn of luck, it was Mark.

"What's up?"

"A political exposé, possibly. But I don't want to go into any more details yet."

"Okay. I'll wait to hear from you."

"Talk to you later."

Mark disconnected the line. There was hope of an escape from Thunder Canyon without quitting his job. Hope of a story that was worthy of his skill.

So why didn't that make him feel better?

He strode over to the honor bar in his room, unlocked the door and fished out a bottle of bourbon. Taking a glass from the bathroom, he made a stiff drink, using just a splash of water—his usual beverage of escape.

But this time, it wasn't memories of his sister that made him want to drown his sorrows. It was thoughts of a petite brunette with a Latin temper and a fiery kiss that he might never taste again.

A hot-blooded woman who had a death-grip hold on him and made the squeeze feel comfortable. Appealing.

And that scary thought was enough to make him want to jump in a vat of bourbon and never climb out.

He plopped onto the chair by the desk and took a drink. But the alcohol didn't slide easily down his throat, nor did it hit the spot.

Juliet wasn't going to be an easy woman to forget.

Swearing under his breath, he dumped the bourbon down the drain.

Chapter Fourteen

Over the next couple of hours, Juliet's anger slowly shifted from Mark to herself. She should have known better than to let him get too close, than to have pinned her dreams of love and forever on him.

I hoped we could work out something beneficial for both of us, he'd told her.

On the outside, that sounded like a generous offer. But when he added, *I hoped you'd look after my interests,* her suspicions had been confirmed.

Mark hadn't wanted any more from her than Erik had. And this time the revelation hurt more than it had before.

A lot more.

She'd hoped to stay mad at Mark, and even at herself; anger was so much easier to deal with. But by sunset, grief and loneliness trickled in, burrowing into her heart.

After a light dinner, she spent some quiet time with Marissa, then nursed her and put her to bed.

But that merely left Juliet alone with her thoughts, with her deep sense of loss.

Until a knock sounded at her door.

Uneasy since it was nearly nine, she peered through the droopy drapes. The glow from the single light in the rear parking lot lit a familiar form.

Mark.

She hadn't expected to see him. And although she had half a notion to either ignore him or give him another piece of her mind—a colorful, multilingual version—she opened the door.

"I…uh…wanted to talk to you about something," he said.

"All right." She stepped aside, allowing him in the apartment.

He nodded at the sofa. "Can I sit down?"

"Sure." She waited until he'd taken a seat, then, wanting to leave some distance between them without being obvious, she sat on another cushion.

"I'm going to be leaving Thunder Canyon soon," he said, "but there's something I want to tell you."

For a moment, she wondered if he was going to apologize and tell her he'd been a stubborn fool. That he hadn't realized how much he loved her, how impossible it would be to live without her. But she knew better than to give a loco fantasy like that the time of day.

"You've been open with me, Juliet. And I've kept secrets from you."

She merely stared at him, letting him continue.

"I'm not sure who you spoke to, who told you I was married before, but it was to a woman who wanted something I couldn't provide. A woman whose love began to die after I told her about the part I played in my sister's death."

"I'm not like other women. Not when I care about someone." It was the closest Juliet came to actually admitting her feelings. Feelings, she realized, that hadn't lessened just because Mark had disappointed her, hurt her.

"I hope you're right about that, because I've had a hell of a time living with what I did. And I'd hate to lose your friendship over it."

"Try trusting me," she said.

"I will. Our friendship means a lot to me. And I should have trusted you before, but I'd been on my own for so long, it was hard to let go." He looked at her with such a pained expression, it tugged at her heart.

Had he done something that unforgivable?

"My older sister, Kelly, married her high school sweetheart right after graduation. Daryl got a job selling cars, and they moved to Bozeman. We didn't see much of them, and I assumed they were happy. But a year or so later, after Daryl left her for another woman, Kelly came home heartbroken and five months pregnant."

Pregnant and betrayed.

Juliet knew the feeling well.

"My sister was miserable and cried all the time," Mark said. "She spent day after day sulking in her bedroom, with the door shut and the drapes drawn."

Juliet had been hurt, too, but she'd been able to cope with her situation. "It sounds as though your sister was suffering from some serious depression and needed professional help."

"You're right. Unfortunately, she didn't get help."

"Not even from her obstetrician?"

"I don't think she saw a doctor after coming back home. My parents were so busy at work that they didn't force the issue. In fact, I don't think they knew how much time Kelly spent locked in her room." Mark leaned forward, resting his arms on his thighs, his hands clasped together. "I knew, though. And I probably should have made a bigger deal out of it."

"How old were you?" Juliet asked, wanting to touch him, to comfort him, but afraid to intrude.

"I was sixteen."

"And at that age, you were supposed to have taken on more responsibility with your older sister than your parents did?"

He shrugged. "In retrospect, I wish I had."

"What happened?"

"One afternoon, a week before she was due to have the baby, my friends were getting together at the bowling alley." He looked at Juliet, his eyes begging to be understood. "You have no idea how boring it was at the house, especially with my sister holed up in her room."

She nodded, wanting him to feel free to continue.

"Before my parents had left for work, they'd told me to stick close to home because there'd been a storm warning. But I didn't plan to be in town that long and figured I'd be back before they got home."

Juliet felt a chill in the room, one that had little to do with the weather and a lot to do with Mark's tense demeanor, his pained expression.

"So I ignored their orders and took the family car into town. Shortly after that, the storm hit even harder than expected, creating a power outage and knocking down telephone lines." He glanced at Juliet, pain etched across his brow. Remorse. Regret. Guilt.

Juliet wished she could soothe them all away, but feared they'd been hiding under the surface for so long that it wouldn't be easy.

"At the time, I didn't realize babies don't always show up on the day they were supposed to. And Kelly went into labor when no one was home."

Juliet had the urge to slide closer, but was afraid to move, afraid to stop the flow of his memory. Still, she reached for his hand, felt a cool chill to his skin.

"When the roads were clear, my parents returned home and found Kelly on the floor in a pool of blood. Dead. The baby was still inside her."

Grief settled over Juliet's heart—for the loss of the young mother she'd never met, the child struggling to be born, the parents who walked into their home and found unspeakable horror.

And for the man who felt responsible for it all.

"The autopsy said the placenta had attached to the

cervix, rather than the uterine wall. Anyway, she hemorrhaged and died before the baby was born."

"It's called placenta previa," Juliet explained. In her studies of pregnancy and labor, she'd read about the condition. In a case like that, dilation of the cervix caused the placenta to rip away too soon, leaving the baby without oxygen and the mother at risk for hemorrhage. "With proper medical care, the prognosis is good. A doctor can schedule a C-section."

He nodded, processing her words. Or so she hoped.

Juliet gave his hand a squeeze, hoping to chase away the chill, the undeserved guilt he'd carried for years. "Your sister's death wasn't your fault. It was hers. And if she'd been too depressed to see to her own health and that of the baby, it was your parents' fault for not insisting she get the help she needed."

Just hearing Juliet absolve him from guilt helped, Mark supposed. But he still wished he would have done something, gotten Kelly to seek medical care, counseling. Something. And he wished he hadn't left her alone.

"When I finally returned home, my parents lashed out at me, blaming me for leaving my sister alone, for being so selfish and irresponsible." Mark didn't tell her the rest, the words her father had shouted as he slammed his fist into the wall, leaving a knuckle-bruising hole. A hole his old man had refused to seal up for the next six months as a constant reminder of what he thought of his son.

You no good rebellious bastard. You son of a bitch. You let your sister die. You killed her.

I didn't know she was in labor, Mark had tried to explain. *I didn't know she would need help.*

You were told to stay home and look after her. Jess Anderson paced the floor, looking like a madman. *Get the hell out of my house. And don't ever come back.*

"Kelly's death wasn't your fault," Juliet repeated. "And your parents know that. *Now.*"

"I was devastated by my sister's death. And wracked with guilt. And there wasn't a damn person in the world to talk to."

Juliet slid closer, then wrapped her arms around him.

Mark wanted so badly to lean into her embrace, to absorb her strength, her forgiveness.

For a moment, he gave in and clung to her. But that didn't change the fact that he wasn't a family man. That he was leaving on assignment soon.

And it was better that way. Really.

"Your parents are sorry about blaming you," Juliet repeated.

Maybe they were. But Mark wasn't sure he'd forgiven himself. Still, some of the things Juliet had said made sense. His sister's depression had gone untreated, and she'd neglected to see an obstetrician, at least after she'd moved home.

When it came time to deal out the guilt, there seemed to be a lot of players to consider. He didn't have to take the brunt of it alone.

"You're a good man." Juliet stroked his forearm, trying, he supposed, to soothe his conscience.

It worked. Her belief in him was like a healing balm.

She lifted her hand, placed it on his cheek. "I love you."

Her words blindsided him, causing his heart to race and a response to lodge in his throat. He merely looked at her, amazed. Unsure. Unbelieving.

"I don't expect anything from you," she added, as her hand slowly lowered, leaving his cheek cold. Empty. "I appreciate all you did for me and the baby. And no matter where you are, no matter what the assignment, I want you to know that Marissa and I will always be in your corner."

"Thanks." His voice came out raw. Hoarse. Laden with all kinds of things he couldn't put his finger on. Things her words had unleashed.

I love you.

What did she mean by that?

Did she love him like a friend?

Or was she *in* love with him?

He didn't know. Nor could he figure out why it seemed to matter. In the past, if one of his lovers got starry-eyed, he knew it was time to skedaddle. To turn heart and run. And now seemed like that time.

"I'm going on a new assignment soon," he said. "I'm just waiting to hear the details."

There. He'd done it. Cut bait. All he had to do was go.

"I know how much your job means to you," she said, her voice coming out soft and whispery. "And how much you disliked being in Thunder Canyon. I'm happy for you."

Was she?

"Thanks," he said. "I'm glad you understand. And that you're okay with my leaving."

She leaned toward him and placed a kiss on his cheek. "I wish you the best of luck."

He nodded, not exactly sure what was happening.

She was letting him go? With her blessing?

He'd tried to set some boundaries. And she'd agreed to them without tears or an argument.

So why didn't he feel like hightailing it out of her apartment and back to his place?

She stood, leaving him alone on the sofa. "Keep in touch, will you?"

Huh? Yeah. "Sure."

Why did he feel as though there was something more for him to say?

Before he got in too deep, before he said something that might screw up a perfectly good retreat, he got to his feet and headed for the door.

"Take care," she said, her voice whisper soft.

"You, too." He let himself out and closed the door.

But instead of feeling relief or a sense of escape, he felt caught up in something. And as he ducked into the crisp, Montana night, hoping to break free from whatever held him, the snare only grew stronger.

Juliet *loved* him?

All night long, Mark struggled with Juliet's admission of love, making sleep impossible.

He'd been afraid to ask what, *exactly,* she meant by "love." Afraid that he would be backed into an emotional corner. Afraid he'd be faced with something he didn't know how to deal with.

And now, as Saturday morning wore on, he regretted that he hadn't asked.

Did she love him as a friend?

Maybe. But friends didn't kiss the way they'd kissed. Didn't reach star-bursting, mind-spinning orgasms in each other's arms.

He stood before the bathroom mirror, looking at the unruly strands of hair that bore the brunt of his frustrated insomnia, and ran a hand over his bristled jaw.

Now that it was over—whatever *it* was—and now that he was able to get on with his life, he wasn't so sure that he wanted to.

Juliet had grown on him. And leaving town didn't seem nearly as appealing as it had last night—before his guilt-riddled confession. Before her unconditional acceptance.

Before she'd mentioned love.

Hell, they'd never even talked about the house he meant to buy. The house he'd planned to let her and Marissa live in.

There was a lot they hadn't discussed, a lot that needed to be said. After all, he was leaving soon— maybe even today.

A political exposé, Tom had called it. An assignment worthy of excitement.

But instead of elation, that rush of adrenaline when a new story broke, Mark felt…

Dammit. He didn't know what he felt, but it sure as hell wasn't excitement. Or happiness.

He was going to miss Juliet.

And her daughter.

Hell, Mark had watched Marissa take her first breath, had cut the cord. Held her.

Held her mother.

And now, the two of them had a heck of a hold on *him*.

That was it.

The trap. The snare.

Mark's heart did a death-defying loop-to-loop, soaring, pumping, thumping. Spinning.

But not on a quest to escape.

Oh, for cripes sake. He'd fallen hard for Juliet—head-over-sorry-ass in love.

Still, the realization wasn't nearly as scary as it should have been.

The only scary thing was packing up and leaving town. Leaving her.

He grabbed his cell phone and called his boss.

"Tom, I've had second thoughts. I don't want to pass the gold rush story on to another reporter. I want to write a scoop on the real owner of the Queen of Hearts mine. A story loaded with history and legend—poker hands, lost and stolen deeds. A story about a crazy old outlaw and a prospector with a gambling problem."

"You sure about this?" Tom asked.

Yeah. Mark was growing surer by the minute. "I don't believe that Caleb Douglas owns that gold mine."

"What makes you say that?"

"I talked to him yesterday," Mark said, pondering something the wealthy rancher and businessman had mentioned. "He's contacting Vaughn & Associates, a P.I. firm, to find the deed and verify his ownership."

"You might be on to something. Go for it. And keep me posted."

"I will." Then Mark disconnected the line. He really wasn't sure who the owner was, but he would soon find out, even if he had to dog the trail of the investigator Caleb hired.

In the meantime, he had a few more calls to make. The first was to Roy Canfield, the editor of the *Nugget*. After all, if Mark was dead set to be a homeowner and a family man, he couldn't very well be traipsing across the country on assignments.

When Roy answered, Mark introduced himself and said, "I've got a question for you."

"Shoot."

"How would you like a partner, someone who could help you make the paper all you want it to be and still allow you to take your wife on an occasional cruise?"

"You've got my ear," Roy said.

"I've got a full day planned, but can we get together tomorrow morning at the newspaper office? Maybe around nine?"

"That works for me," the older man said. "I'll make a fresh pot of coffee."

"Sounds great. I'll see you then." Mark disconnected the line.

Damn, that felt good. And it had been easy, too.

He just hoped his proposition to Juliet went over as well.

Just one more call to make—if he could find the number.

Fifteen minutes after getting off the phone, with his dreams soaring higher than they ever had, Mark headed for The Hitching Post to tell Juliet how he felt.

He sure hoped he hadn't read her wrong, but if he had, he wasn't going to take no for an answer. He'd just have to convince her that Marissa needed a father.

And that Juliet needed a husband.

But not just any husband. She needed *him*.

As Mark sauntered out of the lobby of the Wander-On Inn and prepared to cross Main Street, he was surprised to see how many cars were parked along the curb.

The diner didn't open for lunch until eleven. What was going on?

Unable to quell a nose for news, Mark entered The Hitching Post, rather than slipping around the back. He found the eatery filled with women. Giggles, chatter and plenty of oohs and aahs filled the air.

Juliet sat at a table in the middle of the room, a stack of presents and colorful gift bags surrounding her, while a rosy-cheeked, matronly woman held Marissa, swaying back and forth as though in an invisible rocking chair.

Oh, yeah. Her boss was throwing her a baby shower.

Mrs. Tasker met him near the door. "I'm afraid we're not open yet. Not until eleven."

"Do you mind if I interrupt for a minute?" His eyes locked on the woman he loved.

Yeah. *The woman he loved.*

His chest puffed up with emotions he hadn't even allowed himself to dream about in years.

"Why, I suppose it's okay," the older woman said, stepping aside and letting him make his way through the throng of ladies sipping coffee and pink-colored punch.

In the center of the room, the woman he loved was knee-deep in torn wrapping paper and little baby things. He tossed her a smile.

Juliet studied Mark, his crooked grin, the glimmer of sunshine that lit his brown eyes.

What was so important it couldn't wait? Was he leaving now, this very moment? Was this the only chance he had to tell her goodbye?

She'd managed not to cry last night, when she'd bravely let him go—but only until the door closed behind him. And since tears began to sting her eyes, she wasn't sure she could pull it off again.

"Juliet," he said in a voice loud enough to still the chatter and gain the attention of every woman in the diner. "I've got something to tell you."

She crossed her arms, bracing herself, as she waited for him to drop a bomb.

"I love you."

His words reverberated through the room, jarring the heart from her chest.

"And if you and Marissa will have me," he added, "I want to marry you and be a part of your family."

Emotion clogged her throat, making it hard to respond with more than tears. She swiped at the moisture under her eyes.

Was this real?

She blinked, hoping that, if this were a dream, she'd wake up.

But he continued to stand there, a hopeful look plastered on his face.

"You want to marry me?" she asked. "Are you sure?"

"Honey, since the first time you slid a menu in front of me, you grabbed a hold of my sorry heart and made me feel like someone special, someone worthy."

She swallowed the lump in her throat, afraid to speak, afraid to break the spell.

"I love you, Juliet. I love your rose-colored view of the world, the Latin temper you hide so well. Even your interest in history got a hold of me. Lady, I love *you*—plain and simple. Marry me and make my life complete."

Juliet couldn't hold back the tears, couldn't hold back the flood of happiness. She stood, wrapped her arms around Mark's neck and sealed her agreement with a kiss.

She knew she should hold back, make the kiss brief and discreet. But she was too happy, too much in love. And amidst cheers and applause, she offered Mark all the love in her heart.

When they came up for air, Mrs. Tasker was the first to officially congratulate them. "When's the wedding?"

"As soon as I can get the license," Mark said. Then he looked at Juliet. "If that's okay with you."

"That's fine."

"And you'll have to find another waitress to take Juliet's place," Mark told Mrs. Tasker. "My wife is going to take care of our daughter for a while."

Mrs. Tasker grinned. "I figured as much."

He scanned the crowded room, the half-opened gifts. "How soon will the party be over? I'd like to take you someplace."

"We'll need to clear out of the diner before eleven," Juliet told him.

"Good. We've got an appointment at eleven-thirty."

An appointment?

"Are you planning to go to the courthouse and find a justice of the peace?" She'd always wanted a church wedding. Just a small one, of course.

"We can decide on when and where we want the ceremony over dinner tonight. But I don't want to wait very long, not when it feels as though I've been waiting my whole life. But you deserve more than a few words spoken by a county official in front of a couple of witnesses we don't know. Besides, I thought it might be nice if we invited my parents."

His eyes glistened with sincerity, and her heart nearly burst. Her little family was growing by the minute. "I don't think you'll be sorry about including your mom and dad."

"I'm beginning to think you've been right about a lot of things." He nodded at the seat she'd been sitting in. "I'll let you get back to your baby shower."

As she sat, he grabbed an empty chair and parked it next to hers, looking eager to make that appointment he'd mentioned.

Her curiosity piqued. "Where are we going at eleven-thirty?"

"It's a surprise," he told her, a grin boasting of his excitement, his happiness. His love.

Juliet didn't know what he had planned, but it didn't matter.

The future was an adventure on which she was eager to embark.

After the baby shower, Mark took Juliet and Marissa for a drive, pleased with the surprise he'd planned and unwilling to spoil it.

"Where are we going?" she asked again.

"Just wait and see."

They drove to Ranch View Estates, but Mark didn't stop at the sales office. Instead, he turned onto Wagon Wheel Drive and parked in front of the house Iris Grabowski and her late husband had purchased.

The woman's Chevrolet was parked in the driveway.

As he slid from the rented sedan, Mark realized he'd need a new car—a family-style vehicle like an SUV or a minivan. But there was time for that.

He escorted Juliet and the baby to the front door and rang the bell.

Moments later, a beaming Mrs. Grabowski answered. Mark introduced the women, and Iris let them into a vast living room, just waiting for the furniture they'd need to buy. The focal point was a stone fireplace, with a mantel for Juliet to display her pictures. At least, that's what he figured she'd do.

"Honey," Mark said, "Iris has agreed to sell her house to us. And while we're waiting for probate and dealing with escrow, she's going to rent it to us. We can start moving in this afternoon."

"God works in mysterious ways," the older woman told Juliet.

Mark wasn't sure what the Ol' Boy Upstairs had to do with anything. Mark was the one who'd come up with an idea that would help everyone out, but he didn't want to shake the widow's faith.

"My husband and I had put in a lot of upgrades," Iris said, as she led them into a roomy kitchen with Corian countertops and state-of-the-art appliances.

"The house is absolutely beautiful," Juliet said. "I love it."

"Well, let me show you what was going to be my sewing room," Iris said, as she led them down the hall and opened a door on the right.

Mark stepped into a room with pale pink walls and a white, built-in bookshelf near a window that looked into a sod-covered backyard.

"Pink is my favorite color," Iris said. "But I'm sure you can repaint it white or another color."

"Pink definitely works for us." Mark slipped an arm around Juliet, pulling his wife and daughter close. "It will make a perfect nursery for our baby girl."

"I'm so glad this has worked out for everyone," Iris said. "And I hope you don't mind if I leave you here. I'm meeting a friend for lunch."

"No problem." Mark was eager to take Juliet shopping for furniture, eager to hear what she thought about making this house their home. Eager to be alone with the woman he loved.

Iris handed him the key.

Just like that?

"We haven't signed anything," Mark told her. "But I'm good for the money."

"I know you are," Iris said.

The widow obviously didn't have a mind for business. Mark could have been a flake, trying to take advantage of her.

"You're more trusting than you ought to be," he told her.

The silver-haired woman smiled sweetly. "God wouldn't have sent you to me if I couldn't trust you."

Yeah, well her faith was a lot stronger than his. He took out a business card that had his cell phone number on it. "I'm looking forward to working with your son-in-law and the escrow officer he knows."

When Iris left them, Mark turned to Juliet—the woman he loved—and the baby she held in her arms.

His wife.

His daughter.

His life.

Being part of a family never felt so right.

Chapter Fifteen

On Sunday evening, Mark and Juliet drove to his parents' mountaintop home, ten miles up Turner Grade.

Mark had called his mother earlier in the day and asked whether a visit would be convenient, since he knew how much time his parents spent at the motel.

His mom's happiness had been hard to ignore, and she'd asked if they would stay for dinner.

His first thought had been to decline, but when he'd spotted Juliet packing the last of the boxes for their move, he agreed.

Now, they stood on the front porch of the house he'd always considered a prison. A pot of pink geraniums offered a bit of color to the white exterior of what had once been painted a drab, winter-gray, telling him that a lot had changed. Somewhat bolstered by the woman at his side, he knocked on the newly lacquered door.

His mother answered, wearing a yellow apron and an awkward smile. She started to lift her arms, as though wanting to offer a hug, then dropped her hands to her sides and fingered the material of her apron. "Please come in."

The aroma of pot roast filled the air, mingling with a hint of yeast and cinnamon. It wouldn't surprise Mark if his mother had cooked all afternoon. And the fact that she had, pleased him.

"I'm so glad you brought the baby," she told Juliet. "I'd love to hold her, if it's all right."

"Of course." Juliet handed the precious bundle of pink and white flannel to the woman who'd longed to be a grandmother for years. Twenty or more, Mark suspected.

A look of awe swept across her face, erasing years of stress, as she studied the sleeping baby in her arms. Then she looked up at Mark and Juliet with a smile. "Please, have a seat. Dinner is almost ready. Can I get you something to drink? Iced tea? Milk? I have beer and wine, too."

"I'm fine for now," Juliet said. "But milk sounds good with dinner."

Mark had half a notion to ask for a beer, but decided to face the evening head-on. "I'll pass for now, too."

At the sound of steps coming downstairs, Mark glanced up to see his father. It was the first time they'd laid eyes on each other in twenty years, so he shouldn't be surprised to see how time had put a slight bend to his old man's stance, more lines on his face, more gray in his hair.

He walked with a limp, Mark noticed. A result of the arthritis that plagued him?

His father reached out a hand that appeared a bit gnarled. "I'm glad you came, son."

Mark gripped him gently, but firmly. "Thanks. It's been a long time."

"Too long." His father smiled, then turned his attention to the woman Mark was going to marry. "It's nice to meet you, Juliet."

"Thank you. It's nice to meet you, too, Mr. Anderson. Thank you for inviting us to dinner. I'll have to whip up one of my Mexican feasts and return the favor."

"Please," his father said, "call us Jess and Anne-Marie. And we'd love to join you for dinner sometime, wouldn't we honey?"

His mother, pleasure glowing on her face, agreed.

Still, the past hovered over them, in spite of the awkward smiles and small talk.

"Anne-Marie, why don't you take Juliet into the den and show her what you've got for her," his father suggested.

"Of course. Come with me, dear."

As Mark's mother and Juliet left the room, his dad smiled. "Your mother told me your fiancée was pretty. But that was an understatement."

"Juliet's beauty runs deeper than the eye can see," Mark responded.

"Good. I'm glad to hear it. A wise man recognizes the inner woman early in a relationship."

Apparently, in recent years, his father had grown to appreciate his mother, which was nice to know. His parents' relationship had been strained when Mark was a teen.

Juliet had told him about the conversation she'd had with his mother at the clinic. The news that his father had been having an affair while the family had lived in El Paso had come as a surprise, although it shouldn't have. The signs and clues had been there all along—now that Mark knew.

His dad motioned toward the sofa. "Have a seat, son."

Mark sauntered toward the beige sectional and sat, as the past continued to permeate the room, the air they breathed.

There was no other way, but to face it. But before Mark could broach the subject, his father did.

"I owe you an apology son, one that's more than twenty years late."

"I owe you one, too."

"No," his father said. "You don't have much to apologize for. I had a hell of a temper and a shameful attitude years ago. I had my own demons I was wrestling with, and I took out my anger and frustration on my family. Especially you."

He had. And now that Mark knew about the affair that had placed a dark cloud on the family, he understood—even if he didn't appreciate—why the man had been so angry all the time, so ready for a fight with anyone who crossed him, especially a rebellious teenage son.

But Mark didn't bring up the affair. What was the point? His father and mother seemed to have reached a peace about it.

"When your sister died, I couldn't own up to my failure to look out for her. And in my grief, I lashed out at you, wanting you to bear the guilt that was mine alone. Your sister should have been seeing a doctor. And even though your mom thought we ought to push it, I didn't take the situation seriously enough."

"I've carried a lot of guilt over Kelly's death for years," Mark admitted. "I should have stayed home that day. And I'm sorry I didn't."

"Don't beat yourself up over it, son. From what your mother and I have learned, an emergency C-section would have saved Kelly. But with telephone lines down and roads closed…" He didn't finish, didn't have to.

"You're probably right. But I should have stayed home, like you told me. I'm sorry for being such a rebellious cuss."

"That you were. But, truth be told, you weren't any ornerier than I was as a kid." His dad took a deep breath, then blew it out. "Any chance we could start over, Mark? Pretend some of our past never happened?"

"I'd like to give it a try. Juliet has taught me a lot about love and family. And, if you don't mind being a grandpa to the most beautiful baby in the world, I figure we have a lot of catching up to do."

"I can't think of anything your mom and I would like better than to be grandparents." His dad smiled, brightening his face in a way Mark hadn't seen in a long, long time.

Before they could say any more, Juliet and his mother returned to the room. His mom carried the baby, while Juliet held a colorful array of cloth.

"Look what your mother made for Marissa," Juliet said, flashing some little baby outfits and dresses.

His mother, with a glow of pride, looked prettier and happier than Mark could remember.

"I love to sew," she said. "So Marissa is going to be the best-dressed baby in town."

"And I'm going to build us a playhouse for the backyard," his father added, a grin bearing testimony of his acceptance, his hope for the future. "Just like the one I built for Kelly while we lived in El Paso."

Mark remembered the little white house, where his sister used to spend hours with her dolls. His mom had made red-checkered curtains and placed yellow plastic flowers in miniature window boxes.

The memory, he realized, was one of many he had of the happier times, the times Juliet had urged him to remember.

"I'm sure Marissa will like a playhouse," Mark said.

"That's the plan." His dad chuckled. "Your mom and I hope, that if we make our home appealing and keep our cookie jar filled, Marissa will beg for you to bring her to visit."

"I have a feeling she won't have to beg." Mark flashed a grin at the woman he loved. "Family means a lot to Marissa's mommy."

"Juliet, as much as I hate passing this baby back to you," his mom said, "I need to get dinner on."

"Let me help," Juliet took Marissa from Mark's mother and held her out to Mark's dad. "Jess, why don't you take your first turn at being a grandpa?"

His father's eyes widened and his mouth dropped. "She's so little. And I don't know how to hold babies. Never even held my own till they could walk. Maybe I ought to—"

Before he could utter another word, Marissa was placed in his arms.

"Well, I'll be darned. Will you look at that." He marveled over the tiny girl, his eyes glistening. "She's no bigger than a peanut. And she's got her eyes open. Hey there, Angel, you don't know me yet, but I'm your grandpa."

A flood of warmth filled Mark's heart, seeking out every cold nook and cranny.

He'd been alone for so long, that love and family ties had become foreign. Remote.

But not anymore.

Before Juliet could slip away to the kitchen to help his mom, Mark stood and wrapped her in his arms. "I've got you to thank for making things right in my world."

She placed a lingering kiss on his lips. "Thanks for giving love and family a chance."

Five minutes later, they sat around the old dining room table, where love, laughter and forgiveness chased out the old memories, hurts and resentments.

"I know that we never used to pray before meals," his mother said. "But I feel so very blessed, I think it's only fitting to offer a prayer of thanksgiving."

"You've got a point." Mark reached for Juliet's hand and enfolded it in his. "For a guy who'd once been a cynical hard-ass, I gotta admit, I'm the luckiest man in world. And I have a lot to be thankful for."

Juliet returned the loving squeeze. "We all do."

As they bowed their heads, Mark couldn't help but chuckle.

If the future looked any brighter, he might have to shed his cynical nature and borrow Juliet's rose-colored glasses.

* * * * *

MONTANA MAVERICKS:
GOLD RUSH GROOMS
continues in May 2005 with

CABIN FEVER
by
Karen Rose Smith

A private eye arrives in town to
hunt down the true owner of
the Queen of Hearts gold mine.
But when a freak spring storm
leaves him snowbound with his beautiful assistant,
their sparks just might bring an early thaw!

Available wherever Silhouette Books are sold.

HARLEQUIN® Presents®

Seduction and Passion Guaranteed!

GREEK TYCOONS

They're the men who have everything—
except brides…

Wealth, power, charm—what else could a
heart-stoppingly handsome tycoon need?
In the GREEK TYCOONS miniseries you have
already been introduced to some gorgeous Greek
multimillionaires who are in need of wives.

**Now it's the turn of favorite Presents
author Lucy Monroe,
with her attention-grabbing romance**

THE GREEK'S INNOCENT VIRGIN
Coming in May
#2464

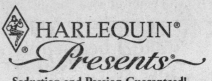

If you enjoyed what you just read,
then we've got an offer you can't resist!

Take 2 bestselling love stories FREE!

Plus get a FREE surprise gift!

Clip this page and mail it to Silhouette Reader Service™

IN U.S.A.	IN CANADA
3010 Walden Ave.	P.O. Box 609
P.O. Box 1867	Fort Erie, Ontario
Buffalo, N.Y. 14240-1867	L2A 5X3

YES! Please send me 2 free Silhouette Special Edition® novels and my free surprise gift. After receiving them, if I don't wish to receive anymore, I can return the shipping statement marked cancel. If I don't cancel, I will receive 6 brand-new novels every month, before they're available in stores! In the U.S.A., bill me at the bargain price of $4.24 plus 25¢ shipping and handling per book and applicable sales tax, if any*. In Canada, bill me at the bargain price of $4.99 plus 25¢ shipping and handling per book and applicable taxes**. That's the complete price and a savings of at least 10% off the cover prices—what a great deal! I understand that accepting the 2 free books and gift places me under no obligation ever to buy any books. I can always return a shipment and cancel at any time. Even if I never buy another book from Silhouette, the 2 free books and gift are mine to keep forever.

235 SDN DZ9D
335 SDN DZ9E

Name	(PLEASE PRINT)
Address	Apt.#
City	State/Prov. Zip/Postal Code

Not valid to current Silhouette Special Edition® subscribers.

Want to try two free books from another series?
Call 1-800-873-8635 or visit www.morefreebooks.com.

* Terms and prices subject to change without notice. Sales tax applicable in N.Y.
** Canadian residents will be charged applicable provincial taxes and GST.
All orders subject to approval. Offer limited to one per household.
® are registered trademarks owned and used by the trademark owner and or its licensee.

SPED04R   ©2004 Harlequin Enterprises Limited

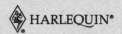

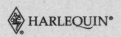

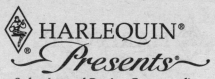

HARLEQUIN®
Presents

Seduction and Passion Guaranteed!

Legally wed, but he's never said...
"I love you."

They're...

**The series
in which
marriages are
made in haste...
and love
comes later...**

**Look out for more Wedlocked! marriage stories
in Harlequin Presents throughout 2005.**

Coming in May:
THE DISOBEDIENT BRIDE
by Helen Bianchin
#2463

Coming in June:
THE MORETTI MARRIAGE
by Catherine Spencer
#2474

HARLEQUIN®
Presents
Seduction and Passion Guaranteed!

**He's got her firmly in his sights
and she's got only one chance of
survival—surrender to his
blackmail...and him...in his bed!**

Bedded by... *Blackmail*
Forced to bed...then to wed?

**A new miniseries
from Harlequin Presents...**

Dare you read it?

Coming in May:
THE BLACKMAIL PREGNANCY
by *Melanie Milburne* #2468